# VORY
## A Charlemagne File

K.A. Bachus

# Charlemagne File Timelines

## Short Story Collection
*A Lighter Shade of Night,*
mid 60s to early 70s

## Novels
*Trinity Icon,* early 70s
*Cetus Wedge,* early 80s
*Brevet Wedge,* nine months later
*Lion Tamer,* five months later
*State of Nature,* early 90s
*Vory,* a year later
*Swallow,* five weeks later
*Quiet Move,* late 90s
*Goat Rope,* 1999

# CONTENTS


PROLOGUE — 1

ONE — 5

TWO — 12

THREE — 17

FOUR — 23

FIVE — 27

SIX — 34

SEVEN — 41

EIGHT — 49

NINE — 57

TEN — 65

ELEVEN — 73

TWELVE — 81

THIRTEEN — 86

FOURTEEN — 91

FIFTEEN — 97

SIXTEEN — 105

SEVENTEEN — 108

EIGHTEEN — 114

NINETEEN — 116

TWENTY — 121

TWENTY-ONE — 124

| | |
|---|---|
| TWENTY-TWO | 127 |
| TWENTY-THREE | 131 |
| TWENTY-FOUR | 133 |
| TWENTY-FIVE | 137 |
| TWENTY-SIX | 145 |
| TWENTY-SEVEN | 151 |
| TWENTY-EIGHT | 156 |
| TWENTY-NINE | 161 |
| THIRTY | 169 |
| THIRTY-ONE | 173 |
| THIRTY-TWO | 178 |
| THIRTY-THREE | 183 |
| THIRTY-FOUR | 188 |
| THIRTY-FIVE | 194 |
| THIRTY-SIX | 198 |
| THIRTY-SEVEN | 202 |
| THIRTY-EIGHT | 205 |
| EPILOGUE | 214 |
| GLOSSARY OF GAME NAMES | 222 |
| GLOSSARY OF TERMS | 224 |

# PROLOGUE

He found her. It had taken him almost ten years, but he had her where she belonged—in his sights.

They were careful to maintain a distance after his father's murder. So careful. And she changed colleges, with no word where. She seemed to drop out of sight, but he knew better. This had the marks of protection. From what? From his father's murderer? No. It had to be from him. From his revenge.

He printed the address, placed it in his planner, called his travel agent, and booked a flight to Florida.

The airplane was crowded, a regional jet out of Atlanta. He sat next to a blond man around his own age, who was packing. It took a practiced eye to know the cut of a sports coat meant to conceal. David Bertram knew because he, too, was armed. He studied the man carefully, in small glances, a snapshot at a time. First the eyes: blue. Scars on the left hand, some of them significant.

He wondered what the man could be. Not *vor*, he decided, not a thief under the code. The man had a Slavic hint about him, but no tattoos. There was a federal prison in Fort Walton Beach. Maybe he was connected to that. David rejected the idea. The coat had cost a pretty penny, too expensive for a civil servant of any kind. David should know. He was the son of a civil servant. A murdered civil servant.

It was the murder that had changed his life. He was seventeen when Nick approached him at the funeral. He became like a father figure, urging him to transfer to MIT, and helping him apply for financial aid from a number of organizations David had never heard of. He never would have been able to manage it otherwise, especially without his dad.

Nick guided him through his graduate work and encouraged him to take his present job working in cyber security for a firm based in Eastern Europe. It meant he traveled enough to know a European coat when he saw it sitting next to him, but the guy spoke American English to the flight attendant. A diplomat maybe? Going to Fort Walton Beach? Maybe the guy was Canadian. David listened for clues, like the use of eh, or his pronunciation of the diphthong 'ou.' He heard nothing, but then, the only languages he had any real facility with were computer languages.

It had been a year now since Nick told David what he discovered about his father's murder, about how Dad's boss had been involved, and not only him but his wife and daughter as well.

David started the search then, once the dust settled after the fracas down in San Antonio that had his office scrambling to protect the company's servers from being crippled by exploits. He scoured the World Wide Web for any information he could find on those three people and found nothing at all, though recently he thought he had them up north, but the lead turned up empty. It was as if they pleaded guilty to his father's murder. Innocent people do not hide, decided David. The Vilsecks were a large family, but most of them seemed estranged from the three he sought. The three murderers.

And now he had her, the bitch. Now he had her. He had long dreamt of fucking her. Now he dreamt of making the experience even more memorable. He would fuck her, and then he would fuck her over.

...

David saw one of Nick's men at the baggage carousel. He was careful not to let on that he recognized him. Nick was lending him one of his teams to assist David on this operation. As a vory associate he had been trained for it, but this would be his first actual use of those skills. He was truly grateful to his mentor for any help he could get but wondered how difficult it could be to kill one old man and two women.

As he stood next to the blond man from the airplane, David spotted his suitcase on the carousel. He set down his briefcase to take half a step forward and grab the bag when a commotion began not twenty feet from them. The blond man remained very still, unimpressed by the hysteria, but David could not help being curious. He squeezed into the crowd and moved toward what seemed to be the center of everybody's attention.

Nick's man lay on the floor, his eyes staring upward, unseeing. David did not see any blood, but he knew death when he saw it. He pushed his way out of the crowd, saw the blond man leaving with just one suitcase, found his own, and looked for his briefcase.

An hour later, after the police interviewed everyone who had been near the scene at the time of the death, after the EMTs took Nick's man out on a wheeled stretcher with a blanket over his face, after David had made a pest of himself at the baggage office, then again at the airline counter, and finally at lost and found, he was handed his briefcase, still locked. They asked him to open it and inspect the contents before signing for its return. Everything was in place.

He called Nick from the safehouse.

# ONE

Theresa Vilseck turned the lock on her apartment door and noted with satisfaction as her alarms, a hair and a speck of paper, fluttered to the floor. Daddy had taught her well. She threw her keys onto a little table next to the door, kicked off her shoes, and took a long stride into the living room.

"Hello, Theresa."

She spun around. "Charlie..." But he was already upon her, wrapping his arms around her and parting her lips with his tongue. His hands migrated to her bottom, pressing her to him, to a rapidly rising erection that she could feel like a beacon of need. She responded instinctively, as she had when she was eighteen. Her bra strap presented no obstacle to him. She noted other things that spoke of the experience he must have gained in nine years, like the command of his kiss, the tweaking of her nipple, the thigh pressing between her legs, and she wondered if the men she had known in that time had changed her also and, above all, if he would notice.

He broke off the kiss, but kept his hands where they were, searched her eyes, and said, "How many?"

"Two," she lied. If pressed, she would mention her least favorites. He was a dangerous man, no doubt even more dangerous than he had been then, and she did not want her former lovers molested.

He regarded her with alarming stillness, and she remembered what could happen when he became motionless.

"And now?"

"No one."

This, at least, was the truth. Nobody could match Charlie, let alone excel him. Her father looked on their liaison back then as a tragedy in his life, a despoiling of his youngest daughter. She considered herself spoiled, not despoiled by what remained the greatest joy of her life so far, forever making her unable to accept a mediocre relationship. Charlie had never been far from her thoughts —and desires.

He resumed the kiss and swept one arm under her legs, lifting her without breaking it off. He carried her into the bedroom, laid her on her bed, and stripped off the barriers presented by her clothing, piece by piece, all while pressing into her mouth with his tongue. She had no opportunity to object, her mouth being fully engaged, and by the time there was a break in the proceedings, other parts of her were fully involved. With one long kiss, he filled all the empty spaces left by an almost nine-year absence, and was still the most exciting thing ever to happen in her life. If anything, his appeal had only sharpened.

When he entered her, he was not as gentle and patient as he had been when she was a virgin. He was insistent and pounding and she gloried in his power.

They lay side by side and were barely finished gasping when he said, "You know, I've been paying attention. I count four significant relationships and one possible affair with a professor. Which two names were you going to give me?"

It took her several seconds to form a reply. "You're as scary as your father."

"I have been told I'm scarier. Which two?"

"What about you?"

He took a moment. "There was a brief infatuation last year. It ended when she tried to kill me."

"That would do it for me, too."

"So, names?"

"Her name?"

"It would do you no good. She's dead."

She had no reply for this.

"And no, I didn't kill her," he said.

"I wasn't...."

"Yes, you were. But we don't have time. Get dressed and pack a bag. We are leaving now."

...

Leo and Maryann could not see the approaches to the house or even its facade. Blindfolded before they deplaned, exhausted and still terrorized by the spray of semi-automatic gunfire across the back of the house they had been renting in the North Country of New York, they were unaware of the time and ignorant of the place where unseen hands helped them climb down the steps. The jet had picked them up at midnight from a small, secluded airfield in Quebec and made one refueling stop in Reykjavik, where they were told not to go outside, not even to stretch their legs. The shades at the windows stayed down the whole flight.

After a short ride on the ground, they knew they had been led inside when a door closed behind them. Blindfolds off, the light of an overhead chandelier made them blink until they could see a large hallway with a parqueted floor at their feet. A wide staircase before them swept upward and to the left. A small woman in her early forties smiled at them through sad eyes. Not exactly a beauty, the woman's brown curls were lightly sprinkled with gray at the fringes of her face, adding a soft attractiveness to her appearance.

"Hello Alex," said Leo. It's been a long time."

"I hope you don't mind if I use your game name, Frank," she said. "It is the one I've always known you by and this being a serious play of the game, I think it appropriate that we remind our-selves of the fact."

She turned to Maryann. "How do you do? Call me Alex. You and I, at least, are allowed our own names. I know you're exhausted, but I must beg you to meet with my husband. You know him as Mack. Once that ordeal is over," she said with a confidential twinkle in her eye, "we can leave Frank behind in the office to talk strategy. I'll take you to your apartment for food and rest. Is that agreeable?"

Maryann nodded dumbly. She had seen the man named Mack slap a woman twice, years be-fore. It happened in her kitchen while she made lunch. She croaked out the most important thing on her mind, having nothing to do with the woman in her kitchen, and everything to do with the chief concern of her life, the safety of her daughter.

"Theresa…," she said in a voice half whisper, half plea.

Alex nodded. "She is the topic foremost in everyone's mind right now. Don't worry. Come with me."

She led them up two flights of curling stair-case and along a wide, empty hallway, its sole decoration a narrow carpet with an intricate pattern. After going through a series of locked doors, Maryann recognized the brilliant blue eyes of the man behind the desk. She was invited to sit but would rather run—out this door and all the others that led them to this office. She wondered if they had landed from bad to worse. Leo usually knew what he was doing and she would have to trust him, but what she knew of the man behind the desk made her acutely conscious of his dangerous power.

"Will you be coming with us, Frank?" asked Mack after acknowledging Maryann with a minimal nod.

Frank said yes, of course. Nothing would keep him from being present to protect his daughter—alone if necessary. Mack's question, suggested he would not be alone. Nine years before, it had been a revelation to Maryann when she learned what her husband had been doing all his career. The name was Charlemagne, not a dead monarch but a team of the most competent and deadly operatives in the business. It should make her optimistic to have such allies, but if Mack thought the team's involvement necessary, more danger stalked their daughter than they realized. Frank blanched, his shiny scalp turning white and his eyes bulging even further from their sockets. Maryann moved closer and touched the sleeve of his coat.

"I retired last year when you sent word that David was looking for us," Frank said. "My successor in The Section is Skosh. You met him during the op at my house. He is very able, but I want to participate."

"Naturally. We will take you with us when we leave for Fort Walton Beach in two hours."

"Fort Walton? In Florida?" said Maryann. "That's where Theresa is. She's a surgical resident there, at the Air Force base. We picked public fights with the rest of the family and tried to make it look like our youngest was with us in New York." She rubbed under one tired eye and noticed with dismay the mascara on her finger. "I'm so worried."

"Would you like to contribute to this operation?" Alex asked her.

"Of course, I would."

"Do you think you can run a household that you do not know, listen to and obey our security experts, and care for the staff and our dependents while we're away?"

Mack gave his wife a sharp look. "I have not decided..."

"But surely this is part of the calculation?" said Alex.

Was her manner just a touch too sweet? Would such a man respond to it? Alex added a coy smile.

*Frank would never fall for that.*

"Maryann has seven children and four grandchildren," said Alex. "She is experienced and knows how to run a household. We can trust her in Vasily's Carpet. And she speaks German."

"We will discuss this later," said Mack, hissing between his teeth.

"I'm sure we will." She turned to Maryann. "Let me ask again. Are you willing to run the house for me?"

"I am." Maryann kept her answer short and definite. She knew there was an argument going on, that she was instinctively on Alex's side, and that the least said gave Alex the most leverage. Besides knowing how to manage a household, Maryann was also adept at managing a husband. She left Alex to it.

# TWO

"Will Alex come with us, then?" asked Frank as the women left the office.

By way of reply, he was treated to the cold blue stare he had known so well for almost thirty years. Mack's hair had turned a bit gray, especially at the temples, but this glare remained undiminished in its power to intimidate.

Frank raised his hands, "I know, I know. It is not my business." He resisted the urge to mimic Mack's Austrian accent. Something else must be at stake here, he knew, or no discussion on such a topic would be taking place. Alex did not leave home often. Did the word 'dependents' mean children? The question gave him an intelligence itch. Did Mack and Alex have more children?

Mack brought out maps of Fort Walton Beach, Eglin Air Force Base, and several of its auxiliary fields, most notably Hurlburt Field.

"The team brought the jet into North America to pick you up," he said. "They are in Florida now. We need you to contact Skosh to arrange a reason for us to be there. It will be after the fact, but we do not want complications with authorities. Jay Turner suggests the Special Operations School here." He pointed to a spot at the western end of the city, just north of the Santa Rosa Sound. "Perhaps one of us could be invited to give a lecture there. Jay says he does not have the necessary connections to arrange it."

"In front of an entire auditorium?" asked Frank, eyebrows raised high. He knew that auditorium, secure only up to top secret, but rarely used to that level, mainly because information with a classification that high did not tend to be shared with so many people at a time. The room was large enough to make the members of

Charlemagne far too well known, and they had been there before. It was long ago, but they were memorable.

"Sergei is already known to the vory," said Mack, reading his mind as usual. "They are the enemy in this operation, so there would be no harm done if they were to notice him. We think they do not know his current association with us."

Frank's blood froze, his bulging, bloodshot eyes wide open. "The vory? I thought maybe it was Bertram, David Bertram, I mean." He heard himself beginning to babble.

"It is Bertram. He has become a vory associate and bears the white and black tattoo. His sponsor is Nikolai Beridze, a thief under the code, now working with Russian intelligence. David has his own team, but it is untested. Beridze has given him another, more experienced team in support. We presume he will be supervising his protégé."

Mack looked at Frank's face and wondered why the man's bulbous eyes did not dry up. They bulged further than usual with this news and were unrefreshed by blinking. He debated snapping his fingers to bring Frank back to the task at hand.

"You will be able to call Skosh from the airplane."

"Yes, yes, of course," said Frank with a shiver.

They traced the possible routes between Hurlburt Field, the hospital at Eglin where Theresa worked, her apartment, and three safehouse sites that Jay Turner, their FBI contact, proposed. Mack produced topographical maps of the area, ordinance surveys, reconnaissance photos, and street-level photos. Lack of sleep interfered with Frank's ability to see fine details through his streaming eyes. He did get the overall picture of way too much highly classified photo intelligence spread across a desk in a place he was sure could not be in the United States. Mack knew how to gather intel; he had to give him that. He stifled a yawn.

"You will want to repack your suitcase now and say farewell to Maryann," said Mack. "We will leave presently and discuss this further after you have slept awhile on the airplane." He pulled a bell cord, producing a butler at the door almost immediately, followed closely by Alex.

Their argument began before the door fully closed behind him, but Frank heard very little of it. Once closed, the thick security door emitted no sound.

He hated to wake Maryann, but could not find his suitcase. She lay nestled in an enormous, canopied bed surrounded by the opulence of a palace.

"It doesn't matter," she said with a yawn. "I would have been angry if you left without letting me say goodbye."

She opened a wardrobe where all his clothes had been organized—by a servant, she said, eyebrows raised to her hairline. Servants had never been part of their experience. They found his suitcase in a closet on one side of the bathroom.

Maryann packed for him, as she had for the past forty years, and they held each other while they waited for whoever would be sent to fetch him. A single knock alerted them. They separated as a servant opened the door and Alex walked in.

"I'm afraid I must move you, Maryann," she said.

"You convinced him then?" said Frank.

She smiled, again with a twinkle. How did her eyes do that? "Of course. Or maybe I just wore him down. Come, Maryann, I'll take you to Vasily's Carpet, explain some of the procedures, and introduce you to the interior staff. There are only three. It's excellent that you speak German. You won't be at a disadvantage."

The two women fast outdistanced Frank, talking as they took a path through the mansion that soon diverged from the one taken by the footman carrying his case. He had been made to understand he should follow the suitcase.

He climbed into an armored limousine and sat across from Mack. Incredible wealth, servants, luxury, and a very angry Mack, eyes narrow and jaw set, as they waited for the wife who had bested him in a private argument and was now late. Frank commiserated silently.

There was a quiet but sharp exchange of words in Russian as Alex sat next to her husband. Frank's Russian was rusty. He had not used the language in over a decade and had difficulty piercing the odd mixture of aristocratic and Chicago accents enough to understand entirely, but he got the distinct impression they were discussing Mack's son, Michael, who operated under the game name Charlie. Frank considered the only intelligent thing Steve Donovan's ex-wife ever said was her description of Charlie as 'son of Satan'.

The operation was shaping up like all the others: danger, uncertainty, and disagreeable associates, but this time, Frank had a personal stake in the outcome.

## THREE

"Dad!" Theresa ran into the arms of the bald man with bulging eyes who stood up when she came into the safehouse. "Where is mom?"

"Safe."

"What do you mean? Why aren't you in New York?" She looked past him as they each stepped back from their hug. Jay Turner, the FBI agent, stood there with a considerable amount of premature gray in his black hair, also Steve Donovan, but no sign of his wife Sally, thank heaven. A man and woman she did not recognize stood close by, and finally Satan himself, Mack. He was the older blond, blue-eyed killer with a talent for stillness, she remembered, and the father of the younger one of that description who held her heart.

"Where is Louis?" she asked.

Silence and dropped glances answered her.

"When?"

"Last year," said her father.

She had only a moment to register her internal regret before Charlie introduced Mara and Sergei Pavlenko, new members of the team. She looked at the young blonde woman before her and again at Charlie. "You are related," she said.

"Mara is my sister."

"And you're on the team?" Theresa was not sure she liked the breaking of this particular glass ceiling. The woman did not look old enough to have graduated high school. Theresa would have assumed Mara acted as some sort of support staff but for the wicked-looking gun hanging in a holster at her hip. Sergei was older than his wife, about ten years at least, with light, almost colorless eyes, a Slavic brow, and a nose that had been badly set after a break or, Theresa suspected, several breaks. He had the same predatory gaze as the other men though, convincing her that the weapon in his shoulder holster also was not a decoration.

Mara smiled without answering. It was as if she knew the progression of thoughts in Theresa's mind. A family trait, along with the stillness in all of them.

Another woman entered the room from the galley kitchen to the right. She wore jeans, a tee shirt, and sneakers in a completely ordinary way, with a cloud of curly soft brown hair, light eyes, and a sparkling presence that was anything but ordinary.

"This is my stepmother, Alex," said Charlie.

A stepmother not much older than Charlie. And wife of Mack? Of course, she could not be ordinary.

"I am so happy to meet you, Theresa," said Alex, taking and pressing her hand warmly. "Or should I say, Dr. Vilseck? Have you finished your training?"

"Please, call me Theresa. I am almost finished with a surgical residency, but I am fully qualified as a physician."

"Splendid. Come in and sit down. Would you like a cup of coffee?"

They gathered at a conference table in a back room of the house, devoid of windows and with steel double doors that had replaced a glass sliding door to the rear. The house was set back from the road on a narrow half-acre of land in an unincorporated section of Okaloosa County. Its keepers mowed all vegetation around it to no more than an inch high to deny hiding places to intruders. The result was essentially a sandlot with a few low patches of struggling Bermuda grass, bordered by decorative neighbors on either side who seemed more fond of vegetation.

Besides the windowless Florida room downstairs at the back where they gathered, the house offered three bedrooms upstairs and a combination living and dining room off the galley kitchen. Another heavily bolted steel back door led from there. The armored front door opened directly into the large living room dominated by a restaurant-sized coffee-making apparatus.

Theresa still did not know why she was there.

Jay Turner began proceedings. It was an FBI safehouse, so he was their host. Frank sniffed a bit with the superior air of a retired member of a sister service with a bigger budget. The unspoken consensus among those who enjoyed this hospitality was that the FBI had put its more limited budget to good use, dependably providing the most important amenities. There were two full bathrooms upstairs and a half bath downstairs. And then there was the coffee.

Jay led with coffee instructions: if you finish a pot, make a pot, to which the more experienced in the room added the silent caveat, unless you are Mack or Charlie.

Theresa knew none of the subtext going on in people's heads and would not have understood it if she did. She noticed that she seemed to be the only person present who had slept the night before. Baggy eyes and coffee jitters were the rule.

"We were unable to find a second suitable house for support staff, so there are nine of us...," said Jay.

"Ten," said Frank, interrupting. "Skosh is on his way."

"What? We don't need another babysitter," said Jay. "And anyway, this is an FBI operation. It is domestic and involves counterintelligence and organized crime. Both lie fully in our wheelhouse."

"I am retired and have no authority to help you," said Frank.

"That's not the point."

"The point is," said a quietly sinister voice at the head of the table, "I make all operational decisions." Mack was leaning back with his coat open. The spotless SIG Sauer gleamed in his shoulder holster, black against a no longer spotless white shirt. He had been without any rest worthy of the name for more than twenty hours now.

"You may resume your bureaucratic bickering when we are dead or out of the country," he said. "Skosh and Jay will behave as a team." He reinforced the finality of the statement with a pointed look at Jay.

Theresa remembered Skosh, a hard man who had worked for her father and was briefly responsible for her family's security when she was eighteen.

Jay resumed a recitation of what he called administrative and housekeeping details. "Women will use the master bedroom and its en-suite bathroom. The men will have exclusive use of the other two bedrooms and the main bath upstairs."

He had begun explaining the watch schedules when Skosh arrived.

Everybody took this disruption as an opportunity to refill their coffee mugs. Theresa noticed that despite Jay's insistence minutes before, absolutely nobody, including Jay, made coffee as the four pots on their burners emptied steadily. All were depleted by the time she reached the machine. Remembering how essential coffee had been to her in medical school, she expected the need to only increase as she filled and restarted both halves of the machine with fully caffeinated coffee, giving the lie to the decaf label on one of them.

Silence reigned in the conference room as she returned, all of them watching the door, apparently waiting for her, judging by the impatience on several faces and the set jaws and glowering looks of Mack and Charlie. It occurred to her that no good deed could provide penance enough for the ultimate sin of keeping Mack waiting.

# FOUR

"We lost touch long ago," said Theresa as the meeting resumed. "Surely David has his own life, like I do."

"David's life now lies with the vory," said Charlie. "Thieves under the code. I sat next to him on the flight he took in from Atlanta. He has the half-black, half-white finger ring tattoo of an associate. Nikolai Beridze sponsors him. One of Beridze's men was also on the flight. They did not acknowledge each other."

Theresa saw the others in the room raise their eyebrows at this. She wondered why they found it significant.

Steve took a passport and wallet from his jacket pocket and slid them across the table to Mack. "A made man and a real threat. Bertram was distressed at the death."

"Are you saying you took him out?" said Jay. "You made a bloody mess in a local airport terminal and didn't tell me?"

"At the baggage carousel, not in the main terminal," corrected Steve. "A new technique I learned recently. Very little blood. Relax. It gave Mara the opportunity she needed to get Bertram's briefcase, and it's one less tango we'll have to kill later."

Mack inspected the passport and wallet and gave them to Skosh, who looked through them and passed them to Jay.

"I think it would be good if you and I met with the local constabulary," Skosh told Jay. "I mean, before more bodies turn up, that is. It's best to have a professional relationship already in place."

"Don't tell me my job."

Mack slapped the tabletop to stop them before they could start and turned to Mara. She brought out a sheaf of photos from an envelope Jay handed her. She gave an overview of the intelligence contained in documents from Bertram's briefcase that she had photographed.

Theresa was still trying to work out the new technique that kills with little blood and decided on three possibilities while contemplating the man with eyes like melting chocolate across from her. She wondered where his silly wife and little boy might be now. Steve Donovan returned her gaze with a mixture of threat and desire that made her gulp and switch her attention quickly back to Mara. She noticed Sergei register the entire silent communication. *Geez, these people say nothing and everything with just their eyes.*

Mara's briefing had to do with a bug planted in the lining of David's briefcase and the need to set up a rotation of listening duty as the tape reels on a machine behind them began to turn. A shabby credenza had been shoved against the wall and burdened with two computers, a printer, and extensive listening and recording equipment. A separate communications station was set up on what looked like an old half refrigerator turned on its side in a corner. The perimeter sensors would sound alarms when breached. Mara demonstrated the separate sounds of sensors at the front, back, and each side of the property. Technology had changed since Theresa sat in her living room wearing a headset to monitor these gadgets. The professional sniping was the same, though.

Also, shoved against the walls of this room and the living room were foot lockers in various sizes, containing weapons, accessories, and the equipment needed to repair, maintain, and clean them. Theresa knew enough to steer clear of these.

She was assigned to a watch like everyone else, always with Mara, Mack, and Jay, and spent most of it on a headset once again, this time listening to David as he spoke to one creep after another, all of it in English because he knew only a few greetings in Russian.

At first, she felt dirty and sneaky and bored out of her increasingly exhausted skull. Then she heard David, in a drinking session with members of his team, presumably taking in more than one bottle of vodka judging from the increasingly boisterous and profane language, describing in lurid detail how he planned to fuck her over when he caught her. It was not the initial description, which was bad enough, but the advice he got from his companions that chilled her, the enhancements to the terror, and finally, the way they spoke her name.

She was a fully qualified physician for heaven's sake, a trained surgeon. She knew about filth and pain and body fluids and she retched over the floor of the conference room again and again until empty of lunch, breakfast, and every molecule of coffee anywhere in her alimentary tract.

Mara helped her up, handed the headset to Jay, took her upstairs, and woke her mother, Alex. Mack woke Frank in the other room, none too gently—out of policy. Alex and Frank tucked her in as Sergei injected a light sedative. She objected but was firmly overruled. Everybody went downstairs to listen to the tape as soon as she was asleep. They did not want her to hear it again.

# FIVE

Mara switched off the tape in a deeply silent room. Frank was the first to speak. He looked at his hands then at Mack. "You son of a bitch. Why do you always have to be so fucking right?" His next target was Jay. "Not a word of 'I told you so' from you either, my friend. I will throttle you if you so much as hint it."

Questioning looks crossed the room as Frank hung his round head in his hands. Steve explained to those who had not been present in Frank's dining room nine years before.

"Theresa pleaded for David's life because he was her friend and only seventeen at the time. He had been his father's accomplice. More than that, he was the instigator of a murder. Misha and Jay argued for a commission on him as well as on his father."

"I should have killed him nine years ago without the commission," said Charlie with a slow blink of hindsight. "I wanted to."

"So let us do so now," said Sergei. "Together with his vory friends."

"We have to find them first."

"This may help," said Mara, who had donned the headphones. "Listen." She reversed the tape and switched to speaker. There was a two-second gap in the drunken revelry. She pinpointed the gap, slowed the tape, and played it again. They heard a deep rumbling drone.

"Air conditioner?" asked Jay.

Steve tilted his head forward. "No. It's an engine. Play it again, regular speed." Mara did so three times until he said, "It's a C-130."

There began a brainstorming game with Steve saying no to each suggestion. Not the airport, how stupid can you civilians get, Skosh? Not Eglin; it's not their mission. It has to be special ops. It has to be Hurlburt Field. As this was digested silently, it was Mack who voiced the suspicion that rose in everybody's mind.

"They have an asset on the special ops base."

"Skosh," said Jay, "is there any progress on getting Pavlenko scheduled to lecture at that school? I appreciate that the invitation allowed us to let them in the country post hoc, but the lecture itself might be helpful."

"A new class started today. I can probably get him in tomorrow or Wednesday. What are we billing him as?"

"A KGB defector, of course. Just don't use his real name," suggested Frank.

"What are you suggesting as a substitute? Igor?" Skosh pronounced it eye-gore.

Frank gave him his roundest frog stare. "Don't take that tone with me, junior. I had to retire. You were the best man for the job, hands down. I couldn't stay forever."

"It's a fucking nightmare, old man. I'm losing all my Asian contacts and haven't had a decent plate of sushi in six months. I blame you for refusing to be immortal. My successor is Korean. How do I supervise him with any semblance of fairness? Tell me that. And I have no fucking idea what's going on in Argentina, nor do I care. You've ruined my life."

"I tire of babysitter squabbles," said Mack in his iciest voice.

"Geez, you scare the shit out of people when you stop moving like that, like an Okinawan habu snake about to strike. Fucking move once in a while. Please." Skosh tried to return Mack's stare until the man's lip turned up at one corner in a half smile making Skosh suppress an involuntary shiver. "Okay, that's worse," he said. "You've made your point. I'll arrange the lecture for tomorrow morning."

...

"I do not know what I am to say." Sergei fidgeted as Mara knotted his tie. "And I must give this speech in English. My English is excellent. I was always getting the compliment."

"No 'the' sweetie," said Mara, "and use the plural. You were always getting compliments."

"Yes, I was. And you have now, this minute, used 'the' with word 'plural'. I do not understand distinction. Also, why do you have such useless things, these articles? They give me the night-mares."

Mara kissed him and he took it as an invitation, extending and deepening the kiss until Frank cleared his throat at the bedroom door. Sergei and Steve checked their weapons again before leaving the safehouse. Jay and Skosh were also armed but not as nervous because they did not feel as exposed as two specialists out in the cold without the rest of their team.

...

It did not go well.

Skosh likened it to letting wild carnivors run free in a shopping mall. It simply should not be done. They were met by a colonel who wanted to know Sergei's name and the topic of his speech.

"Igor Stravinsky," said Skosh. "He'll speak on the historical role of the AK-47 in Soviet intelligence strategic planning."

The colonel nodded, made a note, and showed them to a room where they could wait until the time came to introduce the speaker.

"Igor Stravinsky?" said Jay and Sergei simultaneously.

"It's the only Russian name I know," said Skosh. "What the fuck was I supposed to say?"

"The role of the AK-47? Really?" This from Steve.

"Well, I could hardly say we're here to check out the lay of the land where we have good reason to believe that an asset of the Russian Federation is harboring two hostile specialist teams now, could I?"

They simmered into a low grumble. Nobody sat down. The specialists were decidedly edgy. Sergei paced. Steve unbuttoned his jacket and opened and closed his right hand. As an experienced babysitter, Skosh knew these two were feeling visible and at risk and were showing all the chaotic signs that Skosh's Asian team had displayed on a regular basis. He grew concerned.

It did not get any better. A young woman in a well-fitting uniform came to collect them from the waiting room and lead them to the wings of the stage. Steve gave her a lascivious smile and Sergei smacked him in the arm. They waited off stage while the colonel introduced Igor the KGB defector and Steve tried to talk to the woman in uniform. Jay pushed Sergei onto the stage where he was sure to feel perilously vulnerable in front of an audience of more than a hundred people he could not see because of the lighting. Skosh wondered who came up with this plan. Surely not Frank. Maybe Jay. Must be Jay. *He does not understand the psychology of these guys.*

"Get him the fuck off the stage," he said to Jay. "Now!"

But it was too late.

A voice came out of the crowd, screaming in Russian. Sergei unbuttoned his coat to reach his Makarov. As if connected to his partner by a wire, Steve's hand went to his Beretta. Jay and Skosh reached into their coats. The colonel hissed something about no weapons being allowed in the building. Skosh asked him why there was a Russian in the audience. Foreign exchange, said the colonel. Russians? In special ops? Terrorism, rejoined the colonel, everybody's problem and the wall is down, hadn't he heard?

Steve brought his Beretta fully out of its holster, and translated, roughly, that Sergei was being called a mother fucking traitor to his country. He was just off the stage and Sergei gestured that he should stay there. Sergei engaged his heckler in a shouted conversation in Russian, while Steve translated quietly in the wings.

Sergei invited the heckler onto the stage as he signaled his partner to put away his weapon. Steve merely dropped it to his side and turned so that it would not be visible. After getting the man's name and shaking his hand to check for tattoos, Sergei began a spirited discussion in not always accurate English on what it means to be patriotic, all of it prime bullshit, but the episode ended with a promise by the heckler to share vodka and herring and discuss the philosophical bases of true patriotism at an undetermined place and time in the future.

Sergei buttoned his coat as he left the stage. That he had unbuttoned it was not lost on any of the audience in the first two rows, or on the colonel.

"When did we start letting KGB defectors walk around armed?" he asked.

Skosh shrugged, "Around the time we invited Russian operatives to our special ops courses."

He helped Jay usher their charges out the back door. Steve holstered his Beretta and asked the young woman for her phone number. She responded with a terrified stare.

"Whose idea was this?" demanded Skosh.

"Mine," said Jay as he put the car in gear. "You have to admit it got us on base."

"Couldn't you just flash the magic badge you guys carry oh so proper?"

"That would get me and maybe you in, but they have to be invited, just like they had to be invited into the country."

They—the invitees—were busy checking behind them every few seconds. Another mannerism of wired specialists that Skosh knew enough to be alarmed about.

"Hey guys," said Jay, "as long as we're here, we will ride around for a little while and you can keep an eye out for anything you find interesting."

Given a task to do, the two in the backseat sobered up and calmed down but saw nothing of interest until the car skirted a vast cemented area of hangers, maintenance vans, and military police carrying M16s.

"There," said Steve. "Plenty of places in there. In the hangars."

"But that is a secure area," said Jay, citing the evidence of the M16s.

"Steve would know," said Sergei. "He was Air Force pilot."

So the trip was not a total loss after all.


# SIX


Misha called a meeting as soon as the four men walked through the door. Alex was glad Theresa had recovered sufficiently to attend. She was not happy about the state of her husband. They had met on an operation, the details of which were etched in her memory. The man at the head of the table was not the Misha of home. She recognized instead the operational Mack of her darkest memory, at hazard, efficient, and ruthless. She was always a little afraid of him, but even more when he was like this.

She watched as he quashed another internecine quarrel between Jay and Skosh and then glared Frank into silence before he could come to Skosh's defense. Not five minutes later, Steve and Sergei made insolent remarks when Theresa complained about being the only person making coffee. All Alex could see was Misha's glance directed their way but it was enough. Both men apologized and looked away.

For her, the hardest thing of all, though, was that she had no time alone with him. They had not spoken above a dozen words in the past twelve hours. Each knew the other's purpose in being here, the two missions whose importance intertwined into an imperative that raised the stakes to almost unbearable levels. Both would use cunning and manipulation to achieve their aims, though she liked to think she would be less manipulative. She considered herself nonviolent, while Misha… well, not so much. Their goals required the success of Misha's violence before anything else could have any meaning, a fact she found difficult to reconcile.

They must survive the beginning to have a chance of survival in the end, he told her in his office—at volume and at length.

She agreed and thought she would never convince him about the reality of a thing called future. Then suddenly, he capitulated—without grace to be sure—and allowed her to join him on this trip. Present now in service to the future, Alex watched, listened, and allowed Theresa to make the coffee.

Skosh briefed them on their trip to Hurlburt Field. Alex felt for the man. He had been plucked from a happy job to a hellish one in the run-up to this op. Frank had no choice but to retire, cut all contacts, and disappear with Maryann when the intelligence on Bertram's activities came in almost a year before. Everything that could be done to hide Theresa had been done. It was more difficult for her because professional requirements required that she maintain her name.

"The colonel was not pleased," said Skosh in typical Japanese understatement. When all eyebrows around the table rose at this, he said with some exasperation, "For fuck's sake. They're all special ops. They knew damn well we were packing the minute Sergei put his hand in his coat."

"Especially when Steve drew his out of his holster," said Jay.

"Don't act so superior, Turner," said Steve. "You were ready to and you know it. Nobody could see me anyway."

"All special ops?" said Misha. "The Russian in the audience as well?"

Sergei nodded. "Spetsnaz. Or GRU."

If it were possible, and Alex did not think it was, Frank Cardova's eyes bulged even further than usual from his head. "A GRU—a military intelligence operative on a classified American military course?"

"That particular course is only rated up to Secret, and only in parts," said Jay.

"Only?"

Sergei smiled. "I told you last year when we went after Semianov's list of assets, that you should not be so sure you won the Cold War. When the wall came down, we sent you ever more vory, and now you invite even our technical specialists to your 'only' secret study courses."

"What do you mean ever more vory?" asked Skosh.

"We, I mean KGB, have been sending them at least since the early 1980s. Your immigration did not well distinguish between political and criminal prisoners. When they were released, you often accepted them. They are very patriotic—to Russia. They do as KGB tells them. They are experts at dirt and they live by pressure. They find dirt and exert pressure. Their pressure is for money. KGB's is for information and obedience. They work....," he lifted a hand and furled his fingers, looking toward his wife.

It was Steve who filled in the phrase, "Hand in glove."

"I have managed to neutralize one hundred thirty-six names on Semianov's list of more than two hundred," said Jay. "Are you suggesting there are more?"

"Not on Semianov's list," said Sergei. "But there are more lists."

"As long?"

He shrugged. "Some, perhaps, or longer. We were not the only directorate using the vory."

"Then why did we go after only one of these lists?"Jay said through his teeth.

"Because Semianov included information that would endanger Mara. I do not care what happens to you. I care what happens to Mara."

There could be no better explanation in those nearly colorless eyes.

The Americans in the room, among whom Alex counted herself both by birth and education, sat stunned and silent.

"But Russia is no longer communist," said Frank, grasping at straws. "It's not even KGB now. It's called the FSB and the foreign activities branch is the SVR."

Sergei answered with a smile. "Correct. It is now only a mess and you need not worry." He paused. "Until someone takes power who is both sober and knows how to exploit the assets we developed."

After a short break when dinner arrived, the meeting continued while they ate a starchy meal full of fats and preservatives, catered by FBI contract and eaten with plastic utensils. Questions tabled for further study included how David Bertram was getting access to Hurlburt Field, the possible nature of the asset who arranged to house his teams, that is, male, female, military, civilian, and so on, and how Charlemagne would gain access without alerting any unknown Russian assets in either Jay or Skosh's hierarchies now that Sergei's revelations had sunk home in their minds.

Alex caught herself nodding off and looked up in time to see a tear fall from Theresa's cheek. This would not do. She stood quietly, triggering an automatic response from Mack and consequently from the other men, making them all stand as she led the younger woman into the living room.

"What is it? What's wrong?" she whispered.

"It's nothing. It's silly, and you are so kind. I...."

The tears came faster.

Alex remained silent, looking up into Theresa's tired eyes searching for answers there.

"I left Wooly." Theresa was sobbing now.

"A pet?"

"No. I am so silly. It's just a stuffed animal. I think it was a lamb. I'm not even sure. It might have been a dog. His fur has worn away now. Please don't think I'm an idiot female. It's just that I've had him all my life and...."

"You're tired, my dear. The meeting will be over soon. Why don't you lie down a moment here on the sofa?"

Alex went back to the conference room, entering as silently as possible but managing to catch Charlie's inquiring eye immediately. A lift of her chin told him he was wanted. He lost no time in slipping from the room during a rousing description of Beridze's known tradecraft practices. The exchange was not lost on Misha. Nothing was ever lost on Misha. He set his jaw and narrowed his eyes at her. She gave him a noncommittal smile.

Intelligence professionals populated the room. They noticed all of it.

When Charlie returned a minute later and asked Misha to meet him outside the door, the room heard, in German, "A what?" At volume and even louder, "Are you mad?" Charlie came back in and sat down coolly, while Misha, with a face full of thunder, pointed upstairs and held the door for his wife. Alex knew better than to disobey.

They heard him shouting, then two voices talking, then a somewhat long silence, then an upstairs door opening and footsteps on the stairs.

Steve said quietly what everyone was thinking. "He's had her."

Jay's eyebrows rose.

"No surprise to me," said Frank. "None of them missed an opportunity when they were younger. At least she's his wife. Presumably, he can trust her not to shoot him."

As a blushing Alex resumed her seat, the men became sure of it. She noticed the way Sergei was looking at Mara and knew they had been discussed. Misha sighed and said, "Charlie, tell us what you propose."

## SEVEN

Skosh had been awake twenty-two hours. He caught himself momentarily contemplating a career change from a job he had always loved. Sure, he had skirted a few rules in his time with some of the murdering thugs he had handled in the Far East, but he'd never been this close to it. He wanted to vomit. Only pride kept his cookies down his gullet.

They walked into the conference room where everybody else had gathered. It occurred to Skosh that they were gone only an hour, and the apartment was a twenty-minute drive away. The entire little mini-rescue of a fucking toy lasted less than five minutes, and that included ground reconnaissance.

The two he had begun to refer to privately as 'the delinquents', Steve and Sergei, plopped into their chairs side by side. Charlie came in and found Theresa once again on the earphones. Brave girl, thought Skosh, forgiving her for this most recent shit show. It wasn't like she had anything to do with it other than being the source of misapplied mercy nine years before.

Charlie held the thing out to her while Mara took the earphones.

"Wooly!" Theresa's eyes teared up as she held the worn, faded toy to her chest. She reached up to kiss Charlie's cheek and kept hold of her old toy while she put the headphones back on. Charlie walked behind her back to his seat, turning up the volume of the machine as he went by.

Skosh felt, rather than saw, the silent communications bouncing around the room. He wished he could go upstairs, find himself a bed, and close his eyes for five minutes. Just five minutes. Frank's face broke through his watery gaze. The man's froggy eyes were looking daggers at Charlie as he sat down across the table from him.

Jay spoke first. "How many?"

"Three," said Skosh with a soft belch.

"Do you want to come with me to contact the sheriff?"

"I kinda feel like I've done my part, to tell the truth."

"Are we blown?" Mack asked Charlie.

"No. We used Steve's new method. I think we have more time before it becomes associated with us."

"Tell us."

"They did terrible things in her apartment, destroying her things," said Sergei. "They shit on her bed. It was a pleasure to kill them."

"Except we didn't know about that until after we killed them," said Steve, looking at his friend.

"Then it was a pleasure to have killed them"said Sergei, smugly proud of his tenses.

Skosh watched for signs that Theresa heard what was being said. There were none. The young woman seemed to be asleep with her eyes open. *Must be something they teach you in med school.*

"The toy escaped by being kicked under the bed in their frenzy to destroy everything in sight," said Charlie. "You were right, Papa. They were watching for her. I took one out beneath the stairs. I think he was just a watcher. A big man, though. It's an effective method."

Skosh belched again at the thought of effective methods.

"The other two were sitting in a car," said Steve. "We needed the driver to get out because we didn't want him falling onto the horn or anything, so we had Skosh approach with jumper cables."

"We unlocked a car parked close by and lifted the bonnet," said Sergei.

"Hood, Sergei," said Steve. "Bonnet is British. So when the guy got out to take a look, I took care of him and Sergei opened the passenger door and slipped it to the other guy. Then we went inside and saw the mess in the apartment."

"Charlie found the toy," said Sergei. "Then we left." He slid passports and wallets across to Mack.

"No blood?" asked Jay.

The delinquents shrugged a negative.

"Are you sure you don't want to come with me, Skosh?"

He received another belch and gulp in answer.

"Is this one of those babysitter objections to being too close to it?" asked Jay. "Shit, it was positively brilliant. You should be proud of a job well done."

Skosh was too busy keeping his stomach down to speak. He pointed meaningfully at Charlie and croaked, "His plan."

Frank held his round, bald head in his hands. Probably, thought Skosh, in conflict between gratitude to Charlie for taking out three more bad guys who were after his daughter and thinking of Charlie as a bad guy who was after his daughter.

Mack finished with the passports and wallets and slid them down the length of the table to Mara. She turned around to one of the computers and began typing in names and passport numbers.

"Charlie is correct," she said. "One is a watcher, a rental, American. The other two are Georgian. Not American. I will see if I can find out if they are Beridze's or if he has given them to Bertram. Do we know how many are usually on one of their teams?"

"Six," said Sergei. "Same as KGB."

"This is a new concept to me," said Jay, "at least its political implications, not the organized crime, but their deliberate use by intelligence. I will ask someone I know in DC. There is bound to be an analyst somewhere who has been jumping up and down trying to get people to listen to him about this threat."

Mara turned from her keyboard. "The American belongs to a violent anti-government group with headquarters in Crestview. It is about forty minutes north of here, depending on the roads taken. I have found no other groups or gangs closer than Tampa or Mobile likely to offer rentals."

"Jay, can you make them close down for one week?" asked Mack.

Turner sucked air through his teeth. "Perhaps we can use a firearms charge," he said reluctantly. "They always have illegal weapons, but it has not turned out well for us at times because of reactions in the press. Maybe it would be better if you could."

"I have only one method of dealing with such problems. Your press may find my results extreme and of course, quite permanent. I want only existing rental agreements to end now and no new agreements made for one week. Without attribution of the cause."

"Of course," said Jay. He looked at Skosh, who answered with a glare translatable as 'How the fuck would I know how to do that?'

"We'll be sure to get that done," Jay said, with emphasis on 'we'.

After the shift changed, Skosh joined Jay at the coffee machine to hash out ideas for mission impossible. "You know," he said as he poured coffee into his mug, "if we tell them how their guy died, they might be willing to listen to us about cooling it for a week."

Jay's brow registered scorn and disbelief. "You don't get it, do you? Have you ever lived in the South?"

"I visited southern California a couple of times and I live in Virginia."

"You live in a DC suburb. Let me put it to you as plainly as I can, Skosh. The only people these boys hate worse than the government are blacks and Asians, and guess what we are?"

Skosh rolled his eyes upward and threw his head back. "Together, you and I are all three," he said as his head came back down with a nodding bounce. "What about Frank? He's white and retired."

"What about Frank? Do I hear my name being bandied about for a suicide mission?" Frank poured the last of the last pot of coffee. Alex swept by them, taking the empty pot from him. She returned with a pot of water and poured it into the top, standing on tiptoes. They explained their idea to Frank.

"Sure, I can do that," he said, rubbing his hands together. "I'll do anything to stop thinking too much."

"You can't, Frank," said Alex.

They all glared at her interference. Skosh began to understand Mack just a little bit.

"Have you forgotten?" she said. "It's not just Theresa that Bertram is after. He's looking for you, too, Frank. And you're distinctive, Frank. These people in Crestview could easily describe you. The only thing we have going for us right now is that Bertram doesn't know we're here and that that advantage would be gone."

The three of them stood stunned. Her soft brown hair, dimpled smiles, and besotted knife-wielding killer of a husband had made them underestimate her overall grasp of the situation.

"I am the only one here who is completely unknown and whose description would say nothing. I must be the one."

"The one what?" said Charlie walking up to the machine. He gave her a narrow look as she explained.

"Are you mad?"

"You sound just like your father."

"For good reason!" Charlie's volume rose.

"Think about it, Michael. I mean, Charlie. Even Mara looks like you and would be very memorable in her own right. Bertram did not see you that day, but his mother did and will describe you to him if she hasn't already. I am the only person in this house he has not seen and whose description is ordinary."

Her description might be ordinary, but the woman was anything but, thought Skosh.

"Papa will never agree."

She patted Charlie's arm. "Leave that to me. Is he alone?"

He nodded. "He's gone upstairs. Steve and Sergei are sleeping in the next room."

The four of them stared after her as she climbed the steps. It took five minutes for the shouting to begin.

"What's going on?" said Steve ten minutes later, his voice still groggy with sleep. Sergei stood behind him.

They explained.

"Shit."

"Misha will have very good sex tonight, I think," said Sergei. Then, as the thought took hold, "Where is Mara?"

"Welcome to my world," said Charlie. "My father almost never shouts. Except at Alex."

"Why is there shouting? Is something wrong?" Theresa walked down the stairs, her dark hair standing in knots around her head.

They were too tired to explain again and she was too tired to listen anyway.

She made more coffee.

# EIGHT

They reconvened at dawn. Everyone, except Frank, had enjoyed at least four hours of sleep in the last twelve so that, considering the overall misery of their situation, they were reasonably fresh. Frank felt overjoyed to have made himself useful and relevant for the past two hours, maintaining indoor perimeter checks every fifteen minutes, with the exception of only one room, and outdoor sensor checks—carefully skirting the couple sleeping on the conference table—to check the bar of sensor lights next to one of the computers.

As the safehouse came alive with the waking of slightly less exhausted but hungry people, Jay took delivery of tubs of scrambled eggs, biscuits, bacon, sausage, grits, gravy, and hash browns, and laid them on the conference table in no particular order. There was a discussion about the grits. Some of the Europeans had never seen it. Alex had never tasted it, though she had read about it. She was from Chicago, so the more experienced among them excused her ignorance. They ate on paper plates with plastic spoons because they were out of forks, while Jay tried to explain the difficulties of entering an Air Force base for purposes of a firefight with the Russian mafia.

"It's not just...." He could not conjure a large enough thesaurus to convey his meaning, but tried again. "It's not just the absurdity of the concept. It's the flightline full of eighteen-year-old military police carrying M16s. Those airplanes are classified. Well, the airplanes are older than dirt and used all over the world, but what's inside them is not and Uncle Sam is not about to share that anytime soon. Shit, I'm beginning to sound like Steve Donovan."

Mack tabled the discussion in preference for the task that held first place on everybody's mind: how to manage Alex's meeting with the rental agency. Once again Jay provided initial intelligence.

"They meet every morning for coffee at a diner on the main street of the town. The head MFWIC is a bubba named Earl Smith, age 72, divorced and estranged from his children. He owns a shrimp boat."

"You sure are beginning to sound like me," said Steve.

"What is miffwick?" asked Sergei, voicing the question in everyone's mind.

"Mother Fucker What's In Charge," said Steve. "It's a military title."

The questions they thrashed out included who was going to Crestview, in what car or cars, who should drive, who should be seen, who not, who should stay in the safehouse, who would be in charge of the safehouse, and who would be in charge in Crestview? That done, largely by Mack's edicts because time was pressing, there came a brief argument about how Alex should approach the subject. This was more of a lecture by her husband to her. Nobody argued with him.

"You will make no jokes. You will not smile." She suppressed her smile at this. "You will walk in, sit down, and say what I tell you to say, nothing more. You will not engage in philosophical discussions. You will not speak of morality. You will not tell them their eating is unhealthy. You will not criticize their wearing of hats indoors. Americans do this all the time. You will not say anything about it. You will wear a wire. You will wear a weapon. I told you to bring your weapon. Did you?" She nodded. "Did you bring the holster?" He looked like thunder when she had no answer.

"I have one you can borrow, Mama," said Mara.

Was that relationship in the file, wondered Skosh. Why hadn't he connected Mara with Alex before this? Because Mara looked like Charlie, not Alex.

Discussion did take place over what she should wear. Mack had never noticed what women wore back at his home, let alone in the forests and bayous of the Florida panhandle. Frank and Skosh had the same disability regarding the mysteries of women's clothing, and the height of fashion for Theresa was a new set of green scrubs. Alex had lost all cultural understanding of her own country two decades before and had no experience outside Chicago to begin with. Steve and Jay were sufficiently American, but not sufficiently female to advise on some things, so after Mack ended the argument by banging on the table, Sergei produced a tape measure from his bottomless Footlocker of Useful Things (FUT) and Jay gave the measurements to one of his watchers on duty outside with instructions to go to a local twenty-four-hour discount store for a pair of cheap jeans, sneakers, and a flannel shirt. They cut the sleeves off the shirt because it was summer in Florida, and they rolled the shoes and clothing in sand and a little bit of mud. Until then, it never occurred to any of them to ask advice from a watcher who lived in the area.

The same watcher who advised Jay to roll the sneakers in mud was sent back to the field office and told to bring them his own car, a very used Chevy of no description and doubtful color or cleanliness, but with plain, faded Florida plates and bubbling tints on the windows that obscured, probably illegally, everything inside.

Jay drove. He pointed out that in the South, he would be less conspicuous than Skosh. Steve rode shotgun. Mack and Alex sat in the back. Steve and Mack got out first so that when Jay dropped Alex off a thousand feet from the diner, they were behind her. Jay parked where he had a good view through the diner's big picture window and watched as Alex and then the other two entered. This was Alex's first op in more than twenty years. According to Frank, that first time had been a disaster for her. It explained why Mack was unhinged the entire morning. Frank mentioned that

Mack made all the decisions on that previous op, too.

Jay heard the sounds of people in a diner and turned up his earbud.

"Mr. Smith? Hi, my name is Jenny."

Uh oh. Jay remembered one of the many instructions Mack had given her. *You will stay exactly on the legend we give you. No exceptions. You will not ad-lib.* So much for that one, he thought. She had been made to repeat the name Jennifer three times. She was right though. Jennifer would be too formal in this setting.

"May I sit down?"

Her English was too good. She was too polite. Jay felt the sweat beading on his brow and pouring down his back.

"Sure thing, little girl," said Smith. "Can I get you some coffee?"

"That would be lovely, thank you."

Jay groaned inwardly. *You will not accept anything to eat or drink.*

"Mr. Smith, I have something a little delicate I need to discuss with you."

"These friends of mine are trustworthy. Ain't you guys?"

General grunts of acknowledgment.

"Nonetheless, it is vital that we speak privately."

There was a brief silence, and then Smith said, "Scram, you guys," followed by the sound of chairs scraping the floor.

Jay imagined her smiling at the guy. That was on the list.

"Now what is it you wanna talk to your old Earl about, honey?"

"Do you know a man named Cory Lowell?"

"Yeah, what about him?" Jay heard a note of caution in the man's voice.

"Well, I'm so sorry to tell you, Mr. Smith, that Cory is dead. He died late last night. I am here on a quest to save lives, Mr. Smith. Please believe me when I say that in all sincerity."

She had begun to sound a little bit southern. *You will not use dialect or accent like you are an actress in a bad American movie.*

"How so?" said Smith.

"I heard that Cory was working for somebody else when he died and that he was on loan from you. I don't think that's a good idea, do you?"

"I think that's my business, little girl." He sounded hostile.

"I agree entirely, Mr. Smith. But I think in this instance, it might not be the best business to be in. I think maybe you shouldn't be lending anything more to those people, and I'll bet your folks who are already down there will feel a lot safer coming back home after what happened last night."

"I don't know nothing about what happened last night. If this is a threat, I want to know who sent you and I aim to find that out right now."

Jay saw Mack stand up from his seat at a booth in the window. Alex was in a back room.

"I am not threatening you or anybody, Mr. Smith. As I said, I only want to save lives. Please believe that. As a mark of my good intentions, I will tell you something important so you can check with the sheriff's office to see if it's true before you make your decision. Cory died because somebody stuck a stiletto between his ribs and into his heart. I appreciate your time sir, and I'll be on my way."

She wasn't supposed to tell him the manner of death. She wasn't supposed to know the manner of death.

"Now hold on there!"

But she was already at the door, and two men, who were slowly leaving the diner at the same time, blocked Earl Smith's effort to catch up with her.

...

"What're they doing?" Steve murmured through the side of his mouth.

Jay checked the backseat in the rearview mirror. "Kissing," he said, very low, and not moving his lips.

Silence reigned during the hour it took to safely reach the safehouse without a tail while Skosh covered their backs.

# NINE

Charlie looked up from the rifle components spread out before him on the conference room table. Mara sat at the other end of the table reading Vogue Magazine and wearing headphones. The reels were not turning, which meant nobody near David's briefcase was talking.

"How did it go?" asked Charlie as the babysitters came in. He began putting the now clean weapon back together.

"Time will tell," Skosh said with a shrug.

Jay followed him in, carrying a fresh mug of coffee and a half smile, which was akin to boisterous laughter for him.

"Time is finite," said Charlie. "We need a break and we need it soon." He popped in a magazine.

"If what she did works," said Jay, "our odds will improve by a third."

"What did she do?" Charlie narrowed his eyes. He chambered a round.

"Broke about a dozen of Mack's instructions. But she made them sound ambiguous and had excuses."

"She learned from the master of ambiguity," said Frank also carrying a full mug of coffee as he took his seat. "Her husband. He'll make her pay, though."

"I imagine that's what he's doing now," said Skosh. He spilled some of his coffee putting the mug down hard when he noticed Mack in the doorway giving him an unblinking stare. He did not know how much of the exchange Mack might have heard and was unpleasantly aware that he had spoken the last words in that conversation. *Damn the man's silent stillness.*

Mack was not yet in his seat when Mara raised a finger. "David Bertram is awake and has a telephone call," she said. She flipped the switch on the external speaker as the tape began to roll.

"You're what?" said Bertram. "You can't. You can't come here. I'm not ready." After a pause, "I have no place to put you for one thing. You'll have to stay in a hotel. No, the place isn't suitable for my mother to stay in. Yes, Kenny set us up in an excellent location, but my guys are pretty rough, Mom. You would not be comfortable there either." Another, even longer, pause from the speaker. "No, I haven't found her yet, but I'm real close. Okay, I'll reserve you a room. Someplace nice. Two? Who else? Oh, her. A double? Is she bringing a boyfriend? Okay, okay already. Actually, that might work out. Two rooms and one's a double. I got it. Give me the flight info and I'll meet you." They heard a knock on the door. "I gotta go. See you soon. Yeah, yeah, bye, love you."

By this time, the conference room was full, and the last to be seated was Alex. Mara raised her finger again and the tape resumed its roll.

"Shit, David," said a voice as the door opened. "Shit."

"Beridze," said Mara.

"What? Tell me," said Bertram.

"It's the fucking Italians. Has to be. That guy—the big one we got from the shrimp guy—he had a fucking stiletto through the heart. I bet that's how the others died, too."

"Others? What others?"

"Last night. Two of your guys. At that bitch's apartment. Fucking dead in their car. And the rental. That really big guy. Remember him? Fucking stiletto to the heart. I'm telling you it has to be the Italians. I thought we had an agreement with them. Fuck."

"My guys? Shit. But we're still good, right? I mean, do we still have enough?"

"Sure, yeah. I'll find some more rentals."

"Why? There're still four more of them, besides all our guys."

"No. The shrimp bastard told them to run, the fucking cowards. Come with me. You need to talk to what's left of your team before they disappear, too. Like the wind. Like the fucking wind."

There was a moment of profound silence. No secrets exist in a safehouse or isolation cell full of operatives in the middle of an op. All relationships are public. They wanted to cheer; they wanted to carry Alex around the table on their shoulders, her victory had been so complete. But they knew about the rule-breaking and they knew how Mack dealt with disobedience in all its forms. None of them wanted to be on the wrong side of him.

Alex blushed and looked down. Mack smiled slightly. The room erupted into applause, having been given license by that half smile.

When the noise died down, Charlie asked Alex, "How did you know?"

"I saw a book Steve was reading for research on a table at home, and I remembered the injury you suffered last year." She shrugged. "I connected them."

Frank polished his knuckles with a superior smile.

"What, old man?" said Charlie, giving him the blue gaze that was somehow worse than his father's.

Frank was tired and retired and overwhelmed by the many personal threats he faced. He never liked this young man in the first place so he gave his best bulging stare with a smile as he said, "You have to expect extraordinary talent in a babysitter's daughter."

They were locked in a mutual glare as Charlie replied, chopping the ends of his words, "I'm all about the talents of a babysitter's daughter, old man."

Frank broke the stare first, seething.

"Jay," said Mack, "we will need Linda Bertram's flight information. His team members will be present to help the son greet her. We should continue to improve our odds. Who is her friend and who is the friend bringing? Can you find the manifest?"

Jay nodded. "I will call the field office and get them started."

"Use the secure phone you installed in the kitchen. I do not want Beridze to know about us yet, or our interest in Linda."

"Are they that sophisticated? I mean they seem like just a bunch of bruisers." Jay realized too late that he had said this in a room populated primarily by a bunch of bruisers.

"Bertram is sophisticated and an expert with computers and telephones," came the quiet purr signaling displeasure from Mack.

"In fact," said Mara, "he has tried getting into our system three times. I don't know if he's been into your system, but as we share a modem ..."

"What?" Mack brought a fist down making everything on the table bounce. Non-team members jumped in their seats. The team was used to it.

"When were you going to tell me this?" he said, well above a purr, to Mara.

She swallowed hard. "He did not succeed. I ordered another hard drive in case, and Jay said...."

The blue mind-reading eyes turned back to Jay. "What did Jay say?"

"I ordered it. It'll be here soon. It was just a precaution; in case we detect anything on your computer."

"On our computer? Have you detected anything on your computer?"

There was an ominous silence. Everybody thanked God or heaven or karma that they were not Jay.

"Um. I am not very good with these things."

"Then get someone who is." Mack was back to the purr, which was infinitely more menacing to anyone who knew him.

"May I point out," said Skosh, not necessarily coming to Jay's rescue, "that most FBI field agents don't have the level of clearance necessary to be here at all, we cannot let him leave once he's here, and we are already overcrowded."

Jay never missed an opportunity to look a gift horse in the mouth. "Our special agents have top secret clearances and take regular polygraphs."

"We're talking SCI clearances here, Jay, sensitive compartmented information with a WEDGE caveat and...."

Mack exploded. "I do not care about your clearances. I will cut the throat of anyone who poses a danger to us. That should be enough to ensure silence. You," he pointed at Jay, "will go to the field office and bring back an agent with computer knowledge and a packed bag. Also, bring two new hard drives, and...?" He looked at Mara.

"A KIV-7. Also a couple of CIKs, a TEK, and a filler."

It was Sergei who produced the technology Jay needed to make a list of these mysterious apparatuses to take with him. The FUT included paper and a pencil.

"I'll just accompany Jay to make sure his computer guy meets at least minimum standards for this situation." Skosh maintained the bullshit as he made his escape, closing the door behind him on the word 'situation,' and caught up with Jay at the front door.

"I'm going with you."

"What for?"

"So I can tell you what an idiot you are. I practically handed you an excuse to give him and you had to get all defensive."

Jay started the car. "You heard him, Skosh. He cares about security, not security clearances. No amount of bullshit was ever going to get me out of this."

"I suppose you're right, but where the fuck is this new guy going to sleep? It's bad enough sharing a room with those two delinquents."

"Delinquents? You mean Pavlenko and Donovan? Very apt. They do belong in juvie. But Mack is right. We need professional help with this. Bertram is a true whiz kid. And nobody is getting any sleep anyway. I know I'm not."

"Mara seems like a whiz kid as well, couldn't she…?"

"I can't put her on an FBI computer, Skosh. Mack doesn't care about such things but the FBI sure as hell does."

"Why are we turning around?"

"I forgot that the caterers will be there with lunch. You'll need to be at the door to receive it while I'm doing this."

Skosh thought for a moment. "Jay," he said before getting out of the car at the safehouse, "is this computer guy kind of junior to you?"

"Yes. Quite a bit junior. Are you thinking what I'm thinking?"

"I'm thinking it would be nice to have some assistance with all the housekeeping in this house of horrors."

"I think, Skosh, that you and I are in complete agreement on this issue."

# TEN

J ay walked in and stepped on a tray of hamburgers.

"Shit, Jay. Watch where you put your feet for fuck's sake," said Skosh.

"There is no place to put my feet. Why didn't you have them put these trays in the kitchen?"

"Have you seen the kitchen?"

"Did you give them the empty breakfast trays so they could take them away and make room?"

"That's FBI shit. How am I supposed to know about that?" Skosh cleared a path for Jay and the new agent to get in the door inconspicuously—if that were possible.

He looked at the young man carrying a large bag of computer parts and a smaller backpack that might have room for a toothbrush. He wasn't a kid, Skosh decided, but he was pretty young to be stepping into this job.

"Hi. I'm John Nakamura. Everybody calls me Skosh." He did not offer his hand because there was no place for the new agent to put down his bags. "Did Jay brief you on the situation?"

"Some," said the young man.

"Not really," said Jay simultaneously. "Some things just have to be experienced."

...

Justin Goodwin's experience began as he ferried food, paper plates, and plastic utensils into a back room filled with a huge table, computers, equipment, footlockers, and armed people, mostly men. A small woman with brown hair made sure everybody had access to the food. There was a tense conversation going on in German. Justin had grown up in a midwestern suburb. He knew the language was German because he took a few classes in high school and anyway, everybody knows that nein means no. This was being said a lot. The noise, the languages, the equipment, and the guns were as far outside his experience as he had ever been.

He scanned the room, trying to understand what he was seeing. It was highly classified. *Got that much.* It looked more squalid than secret, though the steel doors and lack of windows were an indication. His eyes came to an exquisite blonde at the other end of the table and rested there because this, at least, he understood. He also grasped the nature of the stare from the man with colorless eyes sitting next to her. The man pointedly covered her hand with his own, and the communication could not be more clear. Justin's eyes moved on.

Everybody was armed, as was Justin himself. Jay had insisted, though he did not find it comfortable. He preferred weapons of the mind, manipulations of ones and zeros moving at the speed of light. He had skill in that arena, he knew, and his lack of significant prowess with firearms made him more arrogant about the fact, not less. Any brute can pull a trigger.

The logical conclusion, therefore, was that he was in a room full of brutes. They lived by their guns. Most needed a shave. All were coatless and had loosened their ties and rolled up dirty cuffs on their less than white shirts, but their holsters gleamed with polish. The visible stocks of the various weapons seemed to sparkle. These guys pulled triggers on a regular basis, and not at the range.

He could tell that the older man at the head of the table, the blond one with blue eyes, was in charge. Justin sat down as far away from him as he could, between the blonde and the small brown-haired woman.He felt that blue gaze travel his way as it shifted from Jay.

"Um," said Jay. "This is Special Agent Justin Goodwin, our computer specialist."

The man was sizing him up, Justin realized with a shock. He saw the glance move from his hands to the pistol in its holster peeping out from his jacket. Justin was being evaluated not as an engineer, nor as a law enforcement professional. This was a cold assessment of his capability as a man of violence, his capacity in the use of that gun.

"We require first to know if Bertram has succeeded in examining your computer," the man said to him in English heavily laced with a German accent. "Then you must guard against his intrusion. Finally, I need all the information you can retrieve about several people."

There were more instructions. Justin wondered if he should get his notebook and take notes or was he expected to remember all these impossible foreign names? Getting the notebook would suggest he could not instantly memorize them and he did not want this man to know that.

"Jay will give you a written list," said the man.

Had he been reading his mind?

"Misha, let him eat his lunch first," said the small brown-haired woman sitting next to him. She spoke English with an American accent.

The guy in charge, whose name must be Misha, pointed toward her with all the fingers of his right hand and an exasperated look. "Alex, we have discussed this."

Justin noticed that everyone stopped eating. The woman lowered her eyes. "Yes, we have. I apologize."

Everybody picked up their forks.

He was about to get up and go to the computer, but she put a hand on his arm, restraining him with a smile. Jay produced no list for him until lunch had ended.

...

Skosh chewed his Western institutional meal slowly, musing upon the education of Justin Goodwin. Not the master's degree from MIT, but the education going on right now in this room as the young agent reviewed the faces of those around him and rested on the pretty surgeon with deep auburn hair and almost black eyes.

After three days in crowded quarters, everybody knew important truths internally without realizing their meanings. They knew, for example, that of all the dangerous men in that house, and Skosh had to include himself, Jay, and Frank in that category—if only to criminals and terrorists— of all of them, then, the most dangerous by far was Charlie. Everybody also understood Charlie was wooing Theresa, and her father, Frank, hated the very thought. He had no choice but to behave himself, because Charlie was among those trying to save her life and because Charlie could kill him instantly without an ounce of compunction. Also universally understood was that the purpose of Alex's presence was to encourage the match so that Charlie might win his fair lady and take her home with him to whatever secure dungeon he infested as the dragon he most surely was.

Skosh amended that last thought. Alex would not condemn anyone to such a fate. Maybe it wasn't a dungeon, and maybe at home, Charlie wasn't a dragon. Maybe. He breathed fire here, though, and Justin, as he encouraged everyone to call him, would be severely scorched if he continued to smile at Theresa like that.

...

After lunch, Justin turned to his computer and stayed busy enough with his long list of tasks that he had no time to smile at anybody. Working on one name after another, he checked off the list until he noticed a change in the noises behind him. He surfaced from the monitor before him and turned around.

The blonde woman whom they called Mara stood shirtless in capri pants, sandals, and sports bra while the older man with bulging eyes secured a wire to her bra strap and into her ear, with a microphone hooked to the bridge between her breasts. He hooked a small receiver transmitter to a belt around her waist. Other pockets on the belt held magazines, a set of lock-picking tools, and a Glock 19 at her back. He helped her slip on a long, shapeless tee shirt to cover the belt.

Jay Turner, his boss, was busy clipping wires to his undershirt, then buttoning a crisp white shirt over it. He had trouble with the buttons. Justin figured he must be nervous. Across the table, the Russian with the light eyes, who had claimed ownership of the blonde and made sure Justin knew it, was being wired up by Skosh over a Kevlar vest. Once wired, he practiced drawing his weapon half a dozen times for a smooth extraction before putting on a sports coat.

The man with brown hair and eyelashes like a girl was already dressed and wired and practicing letting a stiletto drop into his hand from his sleeve. Justin decided he would never mention the man's eyelashes to anyone. Ever.

The two blond men stood by the door in deep consultation. Alex squeezed between them from the living room and spoke to Mara, then gave her a hug. Mack, the name Jay used for the older man in charge of everything, came to Alex and began a point-by-point list in German. She nodded at each numbered item. He blew out an exasperated sigh, noticed Justin, and pointed at him. Justin opened his eyes wide.

"I will cut your throat if anything happens to Alex because of you," he said in English.

"I'll be here, Mack," said Frank.

"You already know that threat." He turned back to Justin. "Also the same goes if something happens to Theresa. Is this clear?"

Justin swallowed. "Yes, sir."

"Jay?"

"Understood, Mack."

"Mara, can you do something to your hair? It is too distinctive."

"Yes Misha, I will make it messy." And she proceeded to do just that, before picking up a cloth bag full of small devices.

"Steve, stop playing. I want to hear each of you first in my ear, then Frank will turn on the main receiver here. Go."

There began a rapid-fire single word from each person who wore a wire, with only one glitch because Skosh had not yet turned on the transmitter at his belt. Mack expressed his displeasure with a curled upper lip. Frank turned on the receiver that sat on top of an old half-sized refrigerator lying on its side and the exercise began again, this time flawlessly. Frank left the radio on.

Mack pointed at Alex. "You will stay in this room with these two at all times."

"Yes, Misha." As he led everyone out she whispered, "Be careful."

# ELEVEN

**"J**ustin," said Alex, "would it be possible to arrange for that hotel where David Bertram reserved rooms for his mother and her friend to not have any other rooms available in case they want to change their reservation?"

"I think so, yes. Why?"

"I remember how funny my father was about hotels. He never reserved a room at all, but he also never accepted the first, and sometimes even the second room they offered. This made it difficult to set up surveillance against him."

"Fred was a master of tradecraft, Alex," said Frank. "He taught me a lot."

Alex smiled. "Nobody brought this up, so I hesitated to say anything during the meeting. I just don't want Mara's work to be for nothing."

"You know," said Frank, "it might be a good idea to leave two other rooms open and wire them as well. That way if they make a change, they will think they've been successful."

"Deviously excellent. But do you think it will put Mara at greater risk?"

"Let's call Jay privately on the car phone and ask him."

The answer was yes let's do it; it will not add risk. They were rolling into the hotel parking lot when Justin gave them the extra room numbers he had allowed the hotel computer to see. "Switching back to network now," said Jay.

"Should that tape be moving?" asked Theresa, pointing to the recorder. "Isn't Bertram on his way to the airport?"

"He must have left his briefcase. It might be ambient noise. Flip the switch," said Frank.

They heard seagulls, then a motor with a low sound, then another.

"Those are outboards," said Justin. "My dad always has a boat on the lake near our cabin." They heard another motor. "I'd say they're coming into a marina or a public slip. Very low power, no wake."

"Justin, find small craft marinas," said Frank. "Is there anything else to narrow it down?"

Theresa donned the headphones and flipped off the external speaker. "Traffic," she said. "Moving fast, so I'd say a major road."

"There is only one major road through this area that is near the water and it runs right by Hurlburt Field," said Alex. "I imagine he would prefer to be near his team if they are on the base. That reminds me, didn't he mention a name when his mother called?"

"Kenny," said Theresa.

"The safehouse will be small, isolated, near the highway, near Hurlburt, and near a marina for small craft," said Frank.

Justin began the search.

Alex watched the monitor from behind him as he worked. "After you find that, can you search for a friend or more likely a family member of Linda Bertram from Virginia named Kenny or Kenneth, who may be military or perhaps a civilian working at Hurlburt Field? Probably someplace near the airplanes."

They reached Jay on his radio channel as he left the hotel parking lot and gave him the address of a house advertised as a short-stay rental that fit all the criteria.

"Shit, Frank," said Jay, "It was made clear to me that my instructions—our instructions—were to take no risks."

"Just look at it, Jay," said Alex. "Mara can assess the risk."

"Misha will kill you, Mama," said Mara, laughing, "and after the loud argument we will know you are making up."

"No! Do they? Do you all…?"

"Do not dare tell him, Mama. You will spoil it for all of us."

"Jay," said Frank, "if this works, call your people and tell them we'll need more machines and tape capacity and some kind of table to put it on."

They began the long wait, no more than ninety minutes in the end, but endless when it stretched in front of them. The only sound was the clicking of Justin's keyboard.

"Alex," said Theresa, "I heard your dad was a babysitter."

"Yes, he was your father's boss."

"A damned good one, too," said Frank.

"May I ask," said Theresa, picking her words carefully, "what your dad's reaction was when you told him you wanted to marry Mack?"

"You should call him Misha now, Theresa. My father died before I married him, but he was not pleased when I married my first husband, Vasily. He was also a member of the team."

"I didn't know you had been married before," Theresa said, confused.

"That is a long story better left for another time, my dear."

"May I ask what happened to Vasily?"

"He died about ten years ago. I will tell you, though, that I have never regretted either one of my marriages. It helped my father to know this about my marriage to Vasily."

Frank made a sound somewhere between a snort and a snarl. Justin stopped typing to listen.

"Were you able to stay in touch with your family?" asked Theresa.

Alex sighed. "Not as much as I would have liked. But I think technology has changed things dramatically. Justin can probably tell you more about secure communications today. I wish it had been easily available twenty years ago."

The radio squawked. "On our way," said Jay. "Success. Switching to network."

...

"It's a good thing I brought plenty of taps," said Mara as she walked into the room not long after. She showed them her depleted bag. "Four hotel rooms and it was indeed his safehouse. I saw the briefcase, so I touched all three of his rooms and the telephone."

"Not good. On our way." It was Sergei's voice. "Open my locker. Tell Theresa."

"Tell me what?" she asked.

"Who?" said Frank into the radio, "what, and how bad?"

"Steve. Several rounds. Collar bone, I think. Maybe more."

Mara opened the FUT and handed Theresa the medical kit. "I'll start water boiling." She came back ten minutes later with a basin of hot water and a stack of clean towels.

Theresa, rummaged through the kit she had been given, "I see some antibiotic and morphine, but no anesthetic. Is it kept somewhere else?"

"We don't use it," Mara said with a solemn tone. "Not during an op. We keep the anesthetic on our airplane. It's reserved for when we are out of the airspace."

"What if I have to do surgery?" Theresa let the shock register on her face.

"We will hold him down so that he will be still for you."

Theresa remembered a history of medicine class from long ago in her training. The professor pointed out that before the advent of anesthesia, a surgeon had to be very sure and very fast for his patient to survive. She prayed she would be sure and fast.

Confronted with the rapidly cleared and disinfected table, she left shock behind her as training took over so that her instruments were organized and the antibiotic drawn up and ready when the team exploded through the door.

This was not the sterile, hushed operating room she was used to. Theresa had seen two similar events nine years before, but she had not been the attending surgeon then, just a kid, helpful but unaware. Everybody was dirty and loud. The patient swore a blue streak, beginning and ending every remark with 'fuck'. She scrubbed up as well as she could and did not want to contaminate her hands. She wondered how she would prepare him without touching him. Just like before, she did not have to. The other men stripped him, not always gently, and Alex stuck the syringe of antibiotics into him immediately.

The noise and disorder were not a hysterical reaction to an emergency. They were purposeful in their actions and knew what they were doing, but it was as if they were on a kind of hyper-drug. Every move was rational, effective, and violent. She watched Charlie tear off the Velcro tabs of Steve's Kevlar vest and remove it roughly. He took out a wicked-looking knife, slit Steve's tee shirt down the middle and through the sleeves, and pulled it from under him, shoving him back down onto the table.

"Fucking stay put, will you Steve?"

"How do you want his arms?" asked Mack, whom she had been instructed to address as Misha. It would be a very long time before she could do that, she decided when she met the man's eyes. He was as wild as any of them. Even her father seemed infected. He seized an ankle and anchored it to the table.

Theresa forced herself to look at the patient. *Don't call him Steve; just refer to him internally as the patient.* She told them to keep his arms by his side but not touching the ribs. Severe bruising covered his torso. The vest had done its job there. At least one bruise over a rib looked bad enough for her to suspect a break, but it appeared to be in place. She touched that place and he winced but the rib felt intact. The major wound was a hole just below the prominent blade of the collarbone on the left side. She repeated to herself the mantra 'sure and fast' and reached for a scalpel before she realized Alex was already handing one to her and doing so properly. Someone had taught her.

Steve screamed obscenities as she widened the hole and the others were no quieter. Now she understood the leather gags they used way back when. She took a deep breath.

"I need you all to shut the fuck up!" she shouted at the top of her lungs. "Especially you, Donovan. I'm not used to patients who can talk. If you want a shoulder when this is done, you have to let me concentrate."

The entry point was not far from another scar, though that one did not look like a bullet wound. It reminded her of the scars she had seen on Charlie's body yesterday. He had none when they first met. It made her pause. How else had he been damaged during these years, she wondered as she inserted a probe.

Somebody fished a tongue depressor out of the medical kit and put it between Steve's teeth. He bit through it and the great straining began. Not only Steve's muscles bulged as his face reddened, but so did those of the men holding him down. But they were all silent and she had the bullet out in two minutes. It took another three to clean and disinfect to her satisfaction. She began the tedious closing.

"He should have some morphine now," said Theresa, looking for the vial she had laid out.

"No," said Misha. "We are live. When we dislodge those tangos from the base we will attack or be attacked. He must be lucid."

"It's not as bad now," said Steve through gritted teeth. "Just get on with it."

Even as he spoke, the new tape machine began rolling and Justin flipped the switch to the external speaker.

## TWELVE

They heard three voices, David Bertram, his mother Linda, and a man they called Nick, older, with a Russian accent.

"Beridze," said Sergei.

"It was horrible, Nick, just horrible," they heard Linda say. "I could tell he was dead, staring straight up like that, but there wasn't any blood that I could see. Then Sally saw him and started screaming and we turned around and there was another one! What's going on Nick?"

"It's the Italians, I swear. And I saw the guy, too, walking out very cool. Nice suit, just like a wise guy. I went around a side door and had a good look. Brown hair, lots of it. Deep brown eyes. Definitely Italian. I let him have it. I could have sworn I hit him. Almost emptied the clip, and would have finished it, but then somebody was coming and I ducked in the doorway and when I went back out, he was gone. No blood. Then the sirens started and I was armed, so I left."

"I didn't fire," croaked Steve from the table, "because I thought then they would know we're here."

"Very good," said Mack. "How is it we are hearing this?"

"We'll explain later," said Alex.

The look he gave her would have made it snow in hell.

Linda was talking again. "Sally is a basket case, as usual. She is such a trial sometimes, but I'm glad I kept up with her, or we never would have known how that horrible family betrayed and killed Richard." She sniffed. "She's told me everything. I think we can use it and her. I'll let her sleep off the sedative I gave her and in the morning tell her it was all play-acting for a movie or something. The boy is with her, which is another trial, but he'll look after her and he may be useful later."

"Danny," Steve whispered.

"You will retrieve him this time," said Mack. "She has broken the agreement." He did not mention the decision he already had made when he learned from his sources that she had left North Carolina.

"She has to go, Mack," said Steve.

"Yes. I will take care of it."

"I should."

"No. She is Danny's mother."

"He won't know."

"Such things never remain secret. I will take care of it. I promised her I would."

Justin thought the sentence should have ended with, it will give me great pleasure, because of the way it was said. He noticed that Jay and the babysitters shuddered.

The table was cleared of medical detritus and Steve sent upstairs to sleep after Theresa had wrapped his chest to immobilize what she suspected was at least one cracked rib. Within twenty minutes, dinner was being quietly consumed as they listened to Linda Bertram prattle on with David about gossip concerning sundry people they did not know. Then she mentioned Kenny.

"That reminds me," said Justin through a mouthful of bland casserole. "I found him."

Forks went down in silence.

"You did what?" said Mack.

"I found Kenny. Alex suggested I look for him, so I did and I found him. He's Linda's cousin."

"Did she? What else did she suggest?" Mack gave Alex a cold stare. Her face was a study in expressionlessness.

"Well, the hotel rooms and Bertram's safehouse."

"His safehouse?"

"Yes, we found it and so Frank called Jay, and then Mara put some serious touches on it, and...."

Frank received the glare briefly, then Mara, then Jay, and it rested finally again on Alex.

"I will speak to you upstairs," said Misha with a kind of softness in his voice that was anything but. He put down the knife and fork and turned to Justin. "You will give Charlie all of this information. Now."

The shouting upstairs was loud. They heard only one voice.

"I hope Steve can sleep," said Theresa.

"It will stop soon," said Sergei. "This will not be long. The information gained is vital."

"She was disobedient. Again." Charlie's voice suggested severe disapproval.

"If you ever...." said Frank, his face reddening.

"What? What will you do?" Charlie looked away and took a deep breath. "He does not hit her and I have never struck a nonoperational woman, old man. Do not insult me in this way again."

As if emphasizing Sergei's point about vital information, Linda's voice on the speaker stopped its prattle and became serious. "Listen, David, do you remember Arkady from the embassy?"

He must have nodded. There was no sound, at least none that rose above the din from upstairs. Justin gave Charlie an empty disk envelope he had used to jot down the information on Kenneth Schott and the address of Bertram's safehouse.

Linda's voice continued. "Well, he sent you two more men. They were on the airplane with us, but of course, we had no contact with each other. We were very careful. They are here in the hotel. I was able to get them into the last two rooms available. I will introduce you before we leave."

Sergei shook his head. "We were focused on the two greeters, not on other passengers. We never saw these."

Mara was in sudden motion as she scrambled to her computer and dug into the bag of wafers, pulling out an index card where she had jotted down names and locations. After some furious tapping at the keyboard, one of the tape machines began turning. She handed the headphones on Linda's machine to Theresa, flipped switches, and they heard a deep rasping voice speaking Russian. A higher male voice replied. Three people present in the conference room spoke no Russian. Two others, Frank and Skosh, spoke some. The team members were fluent. A single word was enough, though, to make both team and babysitters turn pale.

"Komodo," said Skosh, as Alex and Mack came through the door. Alex did not react. Mack did.

"Where is he?" he asked Charlie.

"Here. In the hotel with Linda Bertram. She got him a room there, one of the rooms Alex asked Mara to touch."

"We have a touch on Komodo's room?" Mack's eyes opened wide.

"And his phone," said Mara.

"It is good that we know," said Mack with a half-smile at Alex. "It is terrible that he is here."

## THIRTEEN

What followed would have been a great movie night if the room was filled with friends and if they brought beer and popcorn. None of those conditions applied as a specialist team and their enablers listened in on the private lives of their enemies. They did have coffee.

When necessary, Sergei or Alex translated for those with limited or no Russian. The only person not present was Steve, and no one begrudged him the luxury of extra sleep. Everybody who needed sleep, which was everyone, forgot their exhaustion in the fascination inherent in being unknown listeners to people who think they are speaking and acting in private. It was irresistible.

The new tape machines had arrived earlier and Mara set everything up so that all touches were monitored in real time. The table to put them on did not arrive, so they used the far end of the conference table, making all seats, except Mack and Charlie's, uncomfortably crowded. Nobody wanted to sit too close to either of them.

...

Marathon Movie Night began with Horrors of the Komodo Dragon.

"He is describing me," said Sergei as they listened to the other man who had arrived with Komodo. "He is GRU. Major Gennady Tsaplin, I recall. He says he spoke to the officer in the auditorium. He wants to know who I am and is not stupid enough to think I am Igor Stravinsky. He will not remember me."

You mean you didn't sleep with his wife, thought Jay.

"Who else was in the auditorium?" asked Mack.

Jay was about to use a sarcastic tone to say the audience number when Sergei interrupted, "A young woman named Sergeant Andrews and a colonel called Durring."

Mack turned to Jay. "You must find these two and move them. And their families. Now. Go. Or they will be dead."

It took Jay only a fraction of a second to follow Mack's thinking before he ran to the secure line in the kitchen.

"Gennady is giving Komodo his orders," said Sergei.

Jay took his seat again quietly.

"He is to kill Linda and the boy Danny after they have destroyed the Vilsecks."

"Linda?" said Frank.

Sergei held up his hand for silence and nodded.

"Yes," said Alex. "He did not say Sally."

She turned pale as they listened to the rasping deep voice of the dragon and Sergei resumed the translation.

"He is saying he wants to be allowed to do what he pleases with the young woman. He wants to...."

He could not continue and did not need to because the translation was visible on the faces of the two babysitters with rusty Russian, of Alex, who had covered her face, of Mara whose stoic, inherited icy countenance was not entirely proof against what was being said, unlike the still faces of her father and brother. Their expressions did not change, or if anything, they became more hardened.

"Gennady assures Komodo."

"Komodo presses for carte blanche."

"Gennady reminds him who is boss." Sergei's eyebrows rose. "Ah. He mentions Komodo's sister. He begs to remind him how unpleasant it would be for her to be in prison. How painful for her would be any interrogation. How delightful she would be for the interrogators they would employ." Sergei sighed deeply. "The GRU are not subtle. They should stick to technical intelligence. Such explicit threats ..."

Mack interrupted, with an impatient gesture, a looming discussion of the internecine squabbles in the enemy's camp.

"There is a telephone call," said Sergei, his eyes wide. "Moscow is calling. Gennady says that he understands. The connection is not clear and he has difficulty. We are having difficulty. It amazes me that we needed only to let the Germans bring down the wall in order to make simple telephone calls to operatives in this country, but perhaps there are still obstacles...."

Another impatient gesture cut him short. The room became silent as static interfered with the voice coming over the telephone line into Gennady's hotel room, but the name Beridze was clear enough. His mission had priority.

"Gennady is now speaking to Beridze by telephone in Linda's room," continued Sergei, "and wants David to search the computer for a KGB defector, probably first directorate he thinks. He is wrong.

"Stick to translating, Pavlenko," said Skosh. He received in reply a filthy look as only an operational specialist can give, a look Sergei never dared give his father-in-law Mack. Skosh returned it with interest.

Mara switched the machine back to Linda's room.

"What did Gennady want?" asked Linda as Nick hung up the phone.

"He wants David to find somebody for us. I'll see your boy later and tell him." After a long pause, Nick asked, "The guy who recruited you, was he KGB?"

"Mm hmm," said Linda.

"What did he look like?"

"I don't remember. Just some kid."

"Did he sleep with you?"

All eyes in the room turned to Sergei. He looked away from Mara's cool green-eyed stare.

"No, of course not," said Linda.

"She is lying," said Sergei. When Mara's face turned from ice to fire, he said, "It was my job!"

"Nice work if you can get it," said Skosh. "May we presume she was better looking at the time?"

"Not much."

"You're lying, Pavlenko," said Steve from the doorway. He made Frank move to the other side of the table and took his seat. "You never did anything you didn't want to do."

Linda's voice put a stop to Sergei's retort. "You know I have been only yours since you were assigned to me, Nick. After all, you got rid of the idiot I was married to."

"I did not do that, Linda. You did."

"Those horrible men did."

"You arranged it. I almost did not survive the loss of that asset. He was important to my directorate. You are too reckless sometimes."

"Well, David will be an important asset, now that he knows who to blame. Thanks for convincing Sally to tell him. With any luck they'll take her out, too, and her brat. After the Vilsecks are dead, we should use the kid to trap Charlemagne themselves."

"Whatever you suggest, my love. I am sure we can arrange it. Especially the kid."

## FOURTEEN

When Nick and Linda reduced their conversation to long sighs and low moans, there was a run on the coffee machine and its necessary corollary, the toilets. Frank was the last to return because he had been unlucky enough to arrive at the machine when all pots were empty. Mack had stopped Alex and Theresa from making coffee by edict, a prohibition everyone else found unfair, since neither Mack nor Charlie ever made a pot, and Sergei and Steve made coffee only when they couldn't bully a babysitter into it.

Frank sat down in the smug complacency of a man whose coffee was both hot and fresh. "What did I miss?"

Jay shrugged. "They finished what they were doing and Beridze left." Even as he spoke a reel began turning on a neighboring machine, and Mara turned it to speaker.

"Hello, my beautiful Sally."

"Is that Beridze?" said Steve.

Nobody wanted any part of that question and left it to Mack to answer. He raised one eyebrow in a minimalist form of yes.

"Nick, stop." Sally giggled. "Danny, why don't you go downstairs and get a soda?"

"Mom...."

"Just go. Just for a little while. Go on."

They heard the door slam.

"Come here, Sally. How much time do we have?"

"Maybe twenty minutes. But he doesn't have a key." She began giggling again.

"That is enough time for me," said Nick.

"He's mine," said Steve.

Mack agreed with a slight nod.

They sipped their coffee, taking advantage of the time to attend to ordinary tasks, like cleaning their weapons. Finally, intelligible words again met their eavesdropping ears.

"Sally, I think we will find them tomorrow and we will move quickly. You and Danny must be ready first thing. Wait for me to pick you up."

"You'll kill that awful man who hit me, Nick? You will won't you? Then we can go away and be safe. What will you tell Linda? Do you think she'll be mad about you and me?"

Nobody looked at Steve. They suspected it still rankled him and sensed that he would not appreciate their pity. Those who had never seen Sally knew instinctively that she had to be beautiful to have attracted a man like Steve despite her glaring lack of common sense. They commiserated, but silently.

Mack turned to Justin. "Can you make his research into the KGB defector difficult? Not stopped, just difficult. You have the address of his safehouse."

Justin was about to try explaining the difference between physical and computer addresses when Mara said, "It will be better to place a device at the junction box, but this time not to listen. It would be to interfere with the modem on his line. Louis often listened at junction boxes. I know how to do it if Justin has a device that will interfere with transmissions or perhaps reroute them into oblivion."

"I do, but it's tricky to put on a line like that."

Mack nodded at Charlie. "Take them, now." To Alex, he said, "Bring Theresa upstairs and get some sleep."

Alex opened her mouth as if to object, but closed it again when he narrowed his eyes in an unmistakable command.

When they had left, with a low voice he asked Jay, "Do you have someone reliable in the local office?"

"Ye-es," said Jay, hesitating as though he did not fully trust the question or the questioner.

"Can they hide the boy safely for a few hours?"

Steve looked up. "Misha—"

Mack silenced him with a gesture. To Jay, he said, "Call them on the secure line. Do not use anyone you are not perfectly sure about."

Jay left for the kitchen.

As they waited, Skosh was the first to lay his head on his arms to resume the nap he had begun during dinner. Frank, Steve, and Sergei followed suit. Only Mack stayed awake, thinking, so that when Jay came back at the same moment as the three who had been to the junction box, Mack barked instructions, waking the sleepers.

"You," he pointed to Frank and Skosh, "go upstairs and rest." Justin turned to follow them.

"No. You stay here."

He obeyed and sat down warily. Charlie was in the room. Relations between them, never better than indifferent, had become decidedly antagonistic during the ride to the junction box. Justin took the wheel with Mara as his front passenger and Charlie in the back. As he drove down the highway, he made the mistake of asking Mara's advice on how he should approach Theresa. She raised incredulous eyebrows but before she could say anything, that fucking huge knife had appeared before his eyes so suddenly he nearly ran off the road.

"Put it away, Michael," she said.

"For the millionth time, use the name Charlie." He put the knife away. "I was only helping him think again about approaching Theresa."

"Men don't think at all when it comes to women," said Mara.

"So now you are playing the sage matron?" He paused. "Sergei is not hurting you, is he? He better not be. I saw that hickey on your neck."

"That is none of your business."

"It will be Papa's business if I tell him."

"You'd better not, Michael Joachim. Misha is just being a typical papa. You might consider that when you deal with Frank. Sergei always shows respect."

Charlie snorted.

Squashed back into the conference room half an hour later, Justin made himself as inconspicuous under Charlie's blue gaze as he could become, schooling the muscles of his face into impassivity. He was not fluent but had taken enough high school German beyond nein to understand when Mack asked Sergei if he still had any Russian ammunition. Yes, was the reply. Justin concentrated so hard on understanding what was said that he did not realize the next words were in English and also directed at him. He shook himself.

"I'm sorry, could you repeat that?"

"Can you find a photograph of Kenneth Schott?" said Charlie, slowly, as if talking to a two-year-old.

Justin did his best to keep his temper, but could not suppress a sneer. "Of course I can." This was a pleasure. He knew just where to look, and he had it on the screen in fifteen seconds. Charlie and Sergei stood looking over his shoulder for about thirty more seconds. They nodded at Mack.

"Can they find our safehouse by tracing the computers?" asked Mack.

"Yes," said Justin. "But we can make it more difficult by varying the routing through other cities and universities. I will show Mara how if she doesn't know the technique." He smiled at her hoping he had not insulted her knowledge. She smiled back, briefly, until she looked over his shoulder. He glanced up and found Sergei's glare almost as disconcerting as Charlie's.

He felt like dinner in the big cats pavilion at the zoo, and desperately wanted to go upstairs to sleep. The four men on the team left for god-knows where, taking Jay with them and leaving Mara in charge, with Frank responsible for security. But Justin still had not been dismissed, did not feel safe leaving, and did not feel safe asking. In fact, he did not feel safe, but fatigue became more important than security. He put his head down on his arms and fell asleep instantly. It felt like no more than a minute later when a fist pounded the table just beside his head.

## FIFTEEN

"Call the fire department," said Charlie.

Justin jumped to his feet out of a dead sleep, confused and thinking he was dreaming.

"On the base, stupid. There's a fire in a hangar." To Sergei, standing at Justin's other side, he said, "What number was it?"

The unsafe feeling returned. They stood too close, using the proximity of their mass to intimidate him. He considered himself duly intimidated.

"He said it was the depot maintenance hangar, in the old quality control offices," Sergei answered.

"Call them," ordered Charlie.

Justin sat down and typed a report directly into the base emergency line. Using the modem, he sent it on via San Francisco without including his name. He added a line about many casualties.

"Nice touch," Sergei murmured.

Justin was not fool enough to think the compliment would help him.

They were still there dwarfing him as he hit send. He turned around. "Where is everybody?"

"Sleeping," said Sergei.

"They're out," said Charlie.

He sensed impending violence and knew he was the intended recipient. He tried to stand, but that power was taken from him. Instead, he was raised to his feet, shoved against the wall, and held by Charlie's fist in his gut while the other hand twisted his wrist. He was wearing a gun in a shoulder holster, but couldn't think how it might be possible to get to it, and anyway, wouldn't that escalate things into a handy excuse to shoot him? And who would be the better shot?

"You will not approach Theresa."

"Or smile at Mara," said Sergei with a mischievous smile to Charlie who looked at him with death in his heart.

"A girl like that doesn't deserve a thug like you," Justin said to the man who had him up against the wall.

Charlie worked him over pretty good, adding liberal numbers of bruises to his face and ribs, but Sergei was laughing too hard to help him do it. They both shoved him toward the door smirking, "Go get some sleep. You look like you need it." Mack and Steve were just coming in through the front door. Mack raised an eyebrow when he saw Justin head for the stairs holding his gut, but he said nothing.

"What the fuck happened to you?" asked Skosh when he reached the back bedroom.

Frank's round eyes bulged further than ever. "Let me guess. Charlie happened to you. What did you do, smile at Theresa? I noticed that at least you knew better about Mara and kept her out of your calculus."

Justin could only nod. His lips were still too swollen to speak.

"They're wired now, Goodwin," said Skosh. "The adrenaline is on its way up. They were always dangerous. Now they're fucking dangerous."

"What happened besides your exclusive spa facial?" asked Frank.

Justin mumbled about the device they put in Bertram's junction box.

Skosh left the room and came back with a damp, dirty rag from the bathroom. He handed it to Justin, who declined it, deciding he preferred to stay swollen than add infection to the misery.

"What else?" said Frank. "Why did Mack want you there and us out? What did they say?"

"I don't know what they talked about. It was all in German—way above my head. They asked for a picture of that cousin of Linda's. Charlie asked for it. They looked at it on the screen for about thirty seconds."

"They? Which ones?" asked Jay, who stood in the doorway.

"The delinquents. That's what Skosh calls them. No, that's not right." He squinted to focus his memory. "It was Charlie and the Russian guy."

Frank gave Skosh a frog stare of approval. "What else happened?"

"They went out. They all went out, except Mara. I fell asleep with my head on the table and they woke me up. I don't think they were gone long. And then this." He pointed to his face.

"That's it? No other requests?"

"Oh, yeah. They wanted me to call the fire department about a fire. I did it by computer. Then Charlie beat the shit out of me and told me to come upstairs and get some sleep."

"Why the fire department? What fire?" asked Skosh.

"On the base. In a hangar somewhere." Justin struggled again to remember, but his need for sleep had sapped the ability.

"They hit Kenneth Schott," said Jay. "That's why Mack got us out of the way. This is unacceptable. They even sidelined the babysitters. They don't have carte blanche to hit Americans who are ancillary to the operation."

"Are you telling me my job now, Turner?" said Skosh. "It is part of our normal terms and conditions. Mack's discretion rules, and he does have the commission on both Bertram and Beridze. Anybody ancillary, as you call it, is fair game."

"You really don't want to know what I think of you and your fucking terms and conditions, Nakamura."

Jay had never been this rattled and Skosh was a convenient target for his acute distress. He had ridden in the passenger seat, with Steve in the back as Mack drove them in silence to the hotel where most of their primary targets were staying. In the lobby, Mack directed him to stay behind.

Five minutes later Steve and his eleven-year-old son joined him. They bought the boy a soda.

The transaction upstairs in the hotel was on tape back at the safehouse. Jay heard it when they returned. It filled in the gaps left by his brief interrogation of Danny as he dropped him off in the care of the local FBI field office manager.

Danny had opened the hotel room door at the first knock. Room service took forever and he was starving.

"No, Danny, don't!" said his mother. But it was too late. Mack and Steve pushed in, closing the door behind them.

"Hello Sally," said Steve.

"Hello Dan." Her tone was flat.

"Dan?" said Danny. "Your name's Dan, too?"

"It was," he said. "It's Steve now. You can call me that, or you can call me Dad."

Danny looked at the man's eyes and wondered if the kids had made fun of him for those eyes like they did of his. He had the same eyes, but he still wasn't buying that this was his dad.

"My dad was a terrible person and he's dead."

Sally was about to say something but Danny saw that a warning look from the other man silenced her.

"Well," said Steve, with just a hint of a Texas drawl. "The first is probably true, but the second isn't. Last I checked, I was still alive."

Danny turned to his mother, who reluctantly nodded in confirmation, then back to Steve.

"Dad?"

Steve nodded. "Why don't we go downstairs for a soda? We can talk there while your mom and my friend discuss other business. What do you say?"

Danny looked again at his mother. She nodded numbly, giving him the approval he wanted.

"Danny," she said as he turned away.

"Yes, Mom?"

"I love you, son."

"Me too, Mom."

The door closed behind the boy as his mother looked up into the blue eyes of the man she called Satan.

"Are you going to gut me like a fish like you promised?"

Mack drew out his SIG Sauer and screwed a piston and suppressor onto the barrel, shaking his head. "No. You are still Danny's mother. For the moment."

Downstairs, drinking the soda in front of him took a backseat to Danny's rampant curiosity. He spent most of the time excitedly peppering this man who looked like him with question after question. Some questions, but not many, were answered if he paused long enough between them.

"Why did Mom say you died? Where do you live? Why did it take so long to come for me? How come you didn't call? Did Mom tell you not to call? Or was it Linda? I bet it was Linda. She's bad news, Dad. She wants to kill me. Can I live with you for a while? Can you tell Mom her friends hate me? Maybe she'll believe you."

The unanswerable torrent ended when the other man walked into the lobby and signaled to Steve.

"Let's go, son."

"Where?"

"Mr. Turner is going to take you to a person who will take care of you and keep you safe while I finish my business here. Then we'll be getting on a fancy airplane. How does that sound?"

"Cool, but Mom…."

Jay saw Danny's eyes widen when the other man said, "She agrees that the best thing for a young man is to live with his father."

"Mister, you're not Russian like Nick, are you?" said the boy. "But you have a funny accent, too."

He nodded. "Call me Misha, but I am Austrian, not Russian." He patted a pocket of his jacket. "Your mother has signed the paperwork. That is why she brought you down here. It has been arranged. After you."

He held the door open and Danny walked through it knowing by instinct that his life had forever changed, and for the first time in a long while, he was not afraid.

## SIXTEEN

Jay was about to inform Skosh they would have a date with the local authorities at Sally's room in the hotel next day when Alex appeared in the doorway with Theresa behind her.

"You may want to see this, Frank," she said, then held a finger to her lips.

They doused the light and filed silently out the door to a short gallery railing overlooking the living room. The team stood below, panting and checking their pulses. They had stacked the foot lockers against a wall next to the coffee machine to maximize usable floor space. A table and lamp were missing, probably stashed in the kitchen. The biggest item in the room, a sofa, had been upended and stuffed into the kitchen doorway. The otherwise small space was now sufficiently clear to allow two or three of them to spar in the limited space.

The men were shirtless. Mara wore a sports bra. They had been working for some time and all gleamed with sweat. Alex and Theresa sat on the floor of the gallery in the shadows cast by the downward-directed pendant light hanging on a long cord from a vaulted ceiling overhead. The two babysitters and two FBI agents arranged themselves silently around them.

"Komodo is Kyrgyz," said Sergei. "I was his babysitter on two occasions. He is not pleasant to anyone and is very cruel to his target. He has so many prison tattoos on his face, it is difficult to see his expression, but it is always evil, so there is no need to know how he is feeling. He will telegraph what he is thinking. He is very large, maybe one hundred fifteen kilos, and carries a Yakut knife, about a centimeter longer than Misha's. He screams when he attacks."

Mack brought out his knife. Charlie drew his. They compared, and Charlie's was slightly longer. He handed it to Mack, who put his own away. And immediately attacked, screaming.

Theresa gasped. Alex grabbed her hand and squeezed. Fortunately, the gasp had been covered by Mack's scream.

Charlie defended with a straight arm, blocking the knife hand. Mack corrected the arm to ninety degrees, for power and position. Also, step to the side, he advised. Prepare for him to try again. They practiced at least twenty times and went on to practice different angles of attack. Then they began again from the beginning, adding technique.

"Force his arm behind him," said Mack.

Again, they practiced repeatedly before adding the offensive moves. Alex looked at Theresa's face with concern. Would she be appalled? Theresa winced at some of the more vicious blows but stared at the spectacle with fascination. Then Mack advised his son to cut the man as soon as he disarmed him in a manner that used the natural movement of the act to inflict maximum damage. He should then press in to finish him. Mack gave examples.

"Take him down and cut him," he said. "He has thirty kilos on you. Sergei says it is fat, but fat is useful in a fight. Cut him. Immediately."

Theresa had learned enough German from her parents to understand most of it. Her eyes opened wide at such ruthlessness and Alex sighed inwardly. Theresa must be made to know what she would face as his wife, but Alex prayed she would not turn away in disgust. Michael would not have a better chance than this.

The sparring they saw lasted almost ninety minutes, all of it between Charlie and Mack. The others had toweled off and put their shirts, holsters, and weapons back on before forming a downstairs gallery of their own to sit and watch.

"I know you are all up there," said Mack, still panting from the exertion as he picked up a towel. "You will go into the conference room now and begin listening to any tapes that have been recorded tonight. Take notes, not about what you think is important. Take notes of everything you hear. Alex, I will see you upstairs."

The watchers in the upstairs gallery flattened themselves against  walls as the team took possession of all the upstairs rooms. Mack shut the door behind Alex and began the ritual lecture. Nobody was in a mood to joke about it this time, and Alex followed them into the conference room in less than five minutes, looking solemn.

## SEVENTEEN

"It's been four hours," said Justin. "Why do they get extra time?"

Theresa also wanted the answer to this but did not have the courage to ask. She had never been so tired, not ever, not even in finals week. The tapes had finished an hour before. Skosh promptly put his head on his arms and fell asleep. The man could sleep anywhere. Jay's approach was more dangerous. He leaned his chair against the wall, threw his head back, and snored. Alex curled up on the Footlocker of Useful Things.

"Because pretty soon this is going to end," said Frank, "and if we want it to end in our favor, they must be well rested." He was about to rearrange his head on his arms to force the crick to the other side of his neck when Mack walked in, gazed for only the briefest moment upon Alex, and picked up the sheaf of notes in front of Skosh. They had stripped the printer of its paper.

Charlie and Mara walked in quietly, displaying that unsettling stillness common to their family. In contrast, the delinquents brought all noise and chaos. Sergei punched Skosh's shoulder. "There is no fucking coffee," he said. Jay woke and put the front feet of his chair on the floor just in time as Steve came by. Theresa stood up to make coffee, Mack's earlier edict notwithstanding. She wanted to be out of the room.

"What is this?" said Mack. "I cannot read it."

Skosh looked at the page, trying to focus. "We took turns. That's Theresa's handwriting."

Theresa would have been happier to escape Mack's notice. He pointed to a line on the paper. "My dad said to put down 'no pillow talk,'" she said. "That's what it says. There was no pillow talk."

Mack raised his eyebrows and remained perfectly still, which Theresa had come to regard as a warning.

Jay came to her rescue, yawning. "Nick and Linda are spending the night together. There was no pillow talk. Only an hour of heavy breathing. He snores."

Mack divided the pages among the four other team members, stood by the FUT, and gave Alex his hand to help her up.

"I translated for them," she said, "when the GRU man and Komodo spoke. He is an evil man, Misha."

He nodded.

The room was silent; even the delinquents became still. Mack went back to his seat and the moment passed, another example of the mad operational pendulum swing between boisterous chaos and solemn watchfulness before facing formidable foes.

Jay took delivery of breakfast amid the usual noise, but the team ate very little, concentrating on protein in the form of scrambled eggs, oatmeal, and grits, but no biscuits, butter, or jam. They read the notes as they ate, requesting certain tapes and locations, all provided by Justin so that nothing on his plate was hot when breakfast ended. Theresa saw him look longingly at the food left on the trays and hoped he would have a chance at it before it congealed. Several of the tape locations were replayed a few times. Theresa made no sense of it, but then, she had not had the recent luxury of four hours of sleep, lying down.

Again and again, they heard the snippet of tape in which Komodo, translated first by Alex and confirmed by Sergei, said to Gennady sometime after midnight, "It is a dump. Worse than the last place you put us. Fucking hot and falling apart. Prison rats were smaller than these monsters. I cannot believe they once sold American capitalist crap there. No air. No windows. Only empty, baking parking lots."

Mack sent his icy gaze around the Americans in the room, looking for ideas. Any thoughts at all were tough to come by without sleep. Frank shook his head. Justin stared straight before him.

"I got nothing," said Skosh.

Jay threw his large head back, brought it down again, blinked, and said slowly, "Could it be a shopping center? An abandoned, boarded-up strip mall?"

The other Americans groaned. Yes, of course, that was what it was, crumbling capitalism at its finest as seen by a Russian, with plenty of asphalt and decay. Justin turned to his computer and began a Boolean search for such places in the city, then expanded it to the county. Mara looked for commercial real estate listings.

David and Nick had a few interesting exchanges. Nick seemed irritated with the younger man. David kept pressing for answers. "When will we meet? Should I come to your hotel? You keep saying it will be soon. When is soon?"

"Listen, David. I don't know yet. We are working on some things. Have you had any luck with the computers?"

"No. But we should meet. I need to know when we will move on them. I can hardly see the screen anymore, I'm so tired."

"We cannot move on them until we know where they are until we know who they are. Are you still looking for the Russian who was at the school on the base?"

"Yes, but my Russian isn't good enough for this. I don't think I'm looking in the right places."

Nick sighed through his teeth. "Wait," he said. "Wait. I remember something recent. It was not in my department, but it was in this country. Let me think."

The room, with the exception of Justin, who appeared happy in his ignorance as he tapped his keyboard, stiffened.

"Try San Antonio," said Nick. "Last year. See what that provides."

Two hours later, as Linda and Nick met in her hotel room the tapes rolled and Charlemagne's machines listened in. "David says we are meeting tomorrow morning," said Linda. "He thinks he found where they are, but not yet who they are.

He doesn't think they're Italian, but the location is close to our teams."

"He knows nothing. But the Russian bothers me still. I struggle to remember what I heard about last year."

"When will he be able to attack? He's so anxious."

"I think we will be ready by ten o'clock. We will meet at his safehouse at nine and just walk to our teams to give them their instructions."

"Why not go now?"

"Because we know nothing about them, their numbers, their identities. We need intelligence."

Then as the tape began rolling again, this time live during the team's breakfast, they heard Gennady the GRU man and Komodo as they finished a breakfast pot of coffee laced with vodka in Gennady's room.

"Did you say he has brown hair?" said Komodo.

"That is what my friend said."

"Dark brown, light brown, curly, straight?"

"He said light brown and straight."

"And light eyes? Were they gray eyes, almost without color?

"Yes. Do you have an idea?"

"No. Not an idea. I know who he is. He was my babysitter twice. The bastard would not let me take a trophy. He is Sergei Pavlenko. He killed the best babysitter I ever had, Maximovich, just last year in San Antonio. He joined that western team, Charlemagne, with some guy who thinks he knows how to use a knife. It will be a pleasure to kill Pavlenko. It will be a pleasure to kill all of them."

Simultaneous to this news, Mara pulled the plug on the modem shared by the two computers, and Justin announced, "We're blown." The Komodo conversation had been in Russian, so he did not know he was telling them what they already knew, but he had an instant education in urgency.

# EIGHTEEN

Jay might not speak Russian, but he understood names, he had been in San Antonio last year, and he knew most of the names the team used. The names he heard on that tape meant imminent danger and urgent action. He watched as Frank helped Skosh dress the team with wires and body armor, then tactical vests and belts over black tee shirts and trousers. Alex and Theresa fished clothing and equipment out of lockers. Alex had done this a time or two, thought Jay, or some form of it. When their demands became arrogant and peremptory, she gave back the same attitude without losing time in arguments. The specialists were always the first to break away from her glare. Except Mack. Alex never glared at Mack.

"Justin," said Mara, "find the two lists, yours and mine, that we made of shopping centers. Check if any is within, say, half a kilometer of this or Bertram's house."

Justin had been unconsciously busy gazing at her legs, until Sergei shoved him up against a wall, using a fistful of his collar to cut off his breathing. Frank brokered a peace deal by convincing Sergei to stop wasting time. Justin regained his breath and did as Mara asked.

"Do we have a map of this area?" he asked the room at large. Unfortunately for Justin, the question brought him back to Sergei's attention. Maps were in the stupid FUT.

The preparatory adrenaline rush was just beginning, but the delinquents in particular displayed more than their fair share of aggression, and Justin was an easy target. Skosh bravely tried to stand in their way, but it was Mack who finally called them off.

*"Hör auf!"*

It was as if he'd flipped a switch. They released Justin without serious damage and gave him the requested map. Within five minutes he had the location and was able to give directions. The madmen of just a few minutes before were suddenly all business.

"Which direction does the front of the building face?"

"How large is the parking lot?"

"What is behind the building?"

Jay asked for street names that would make up a corridor between the shopping center and the safehouse, including a generous perimeter. He ran to the secure phone in the kitchen to relay orders for a quiet evacuation and sealing of the area.

When everyone was dressed, all weapons had a round chambered, all FBI and babysitters armed, and even Alex was made to wear a badly fitting Kevlar vest and a holster with her SIG Sauer fully loaded inside it, Skosh asked, "How long do you think it will take them to get here?"

Mack wrinkled his forehead. "We go to them. If we cannot stop them before they come here, they will burn you out. Listen to the radio. We will warn you if they break through so you can try to evacuate. If we have not warned you, do not open the door, but keep watch—and think."

The last two words held a scornful note.

## NINETEEN

D avid Bertram stared at the navy blue water of the Santa Rosa Sound, which he could see through the sliding glass doors at the back of his safehouse. Today was the day. Today he would avenge his father, his poor, stupid father.

He sipped his coffee with satisfaction, gazing southward on a world of sand and water and peace, and so was not prepared for the boom of pounding fists on the front door behind him. It made him jump. He ignored the spilled, scalding coffee staining the tee shirt against his chest as he checked outside and then opened the door.

Nick, Linda, and the GRU guy—what was his name?—Gennady—poured into the safehouse.

"You're early."

"Shit, David, there are developments," said Nick, who went straight to the coffee machine in the kitchen. Gennady followed him.

"Good morning, dear." His mother kissed his cheek. "Is Sally here? She didn't answer her door at the hotel. We thought she might have come here, but I don't think she knows about this place."

"No, Mom, she's not here. What about the boy? We may need him."

"That's just it. She must have taken him with her."

David felt a burn in his throat with this news, like rising bile, as Nick and Gennady came back holding tall mugs. Aside from the coffee, there were no efforts by any of them to become more comfortable even by the simple expedient of sitting down. They stood by the door, sipping, shuffling, grimacing. Linda wore her pursed lip disapproval face that David knew so well from childhood.

He was about to ask about the new developments he knew would raise more bile in his throat, when Gennady volunteered one of them.

"I have moved the teams." Before David could voice an objection, he held up a hand. "It was necessary. There was a fire in that hangar on the base. The fire department came, and the military police. They discovered them. Our men fought their way out. Well, two fought. The rest were too drunk, but not too drunk to remember wire cutters. They slipped through the fence. The two who tried to shoot their way free were killed. I found an abandoned place not far from here. Komodo is with them now. We can still move against Charlemagne at our planned time."

"Charlemagne!" David was new to the game but he knew that name.

"Yes," said Gennady with a smug smile. "Not the Italians. Charlemagne killed your father. Last year, Sergei Pavlenko joined them in San Antonio. Sally's ex-husband was already a member. He is the brown-haired man you shot, Nick. But it seems he walked away."

"But it was a young blond man who came for Richard," insisted Linda. "I remember him. He was not much older than David."

It was this collection of words, each crowding the next into and through his brain, that made David remember the man next to him on the airplane—and again at the baggage carousel. He pictured the dead man. His missing briefcase. But it was found. Everything was as it should be. He had watched the man walk out without it.

He looked at the case on the coffee table, picked it up like it was an alien thing, opened it, inspected it. He took it to the window.

"What is it, David?" asked Nick.

In the morning light, he thought maybe … was the seam glued down? He opened his knife and sliced the lining, viciously, furiously, as they all watched the thin one-inch wafer flutter to the floor.

Even as Gennady broke the intruding tap in half, they were unaware that four more were installed in that house alone, and several in their hotel rooms. But the issue was moot. Though the reels recorded all their deliberations, no one was listening. The babysitters had gathered everybody into the front bedroom upstairs, while Charlemagne systematically destroyed the remnants of David's hopes.

Gennady felt a momentary pang for the young man. He had been a promising prospect but was not likely to live through this. Moscow had been clear. Only Sally was to be preserved. He set off at a trot to find Komodo. Whatever orders the beast could not manage to execute he would leave to the legendary efficiency and competence of Charlemagne. He congratulated himself on a job neatly done.

Ten minutes later, two of Charlemagne's remaining three targets straggled toward the address David had determined was the source of an eerily familiar intelligence behind a computer, or perhaps two computers sharing a modem. He wasn't sure. He set off at a trot, his Makarov tucked into an inside holster at his back. Linda grabbed an AK-47 from Nick's car and followed more slowly. Nick settled into the driver's seat, and said something about bringing the car around, but opened a magazine instead, to take his mind off things while he waited for Charlemagne to do all the work required to rid him of that vicious woman. Too bad about David, but there was no help for it.

...

David was surprised when Theresa came out to talk to him. He thought she had more sense. No matter. He would shoot her and the little brown-haired woman trying to talk sense into her. Not as satisfying as he had hoped, but Theresa would still be dead.

As he drew his Makarov from behind him, he noticed a familiar face in the front window. A nonentity he had known at MIT. That must have been the computer intelligence he recognized. David reserved a third bullet for him. As he brought his sights onto Theresa, he saw the silly little brown-haired woman sight her gun on him. He smiled and then heard his mother's voice coming through the window in front of him, confessing that she had arranged his father's death.

David never heard his mother shout "You bitch!" He predeceased her by less than a second.

## TWENTY

Michael felt useless and stupid. He was not sure about his brother-in-law, Sergei. Standing here, in the back of the building, waiting, he heard the sounds of a brief battle as automatic fire came to him in a rapid tattoo from inside. He was only lightly armored and lightly armed because Sergei said this and Sergei said that, and bloody Sergei put a hickey on his sister's neck, damn him, and God knows where else.

Sergei said Komodo would run out the back and circle to his target.

A door opened, framing a heavily tattooed man lightly clad and with only an AK-47 slung on his shoulder. He ran for a small pine wood behind the building, staying low until he reached the trees, then began picking his way in a westward arc. Michael followed, staying far enough back so that any sound he might make on sand and pine needles would be masked by the big man crashing his way to murder.

He no longer felt stupid. He felt only the intense concentration that would win the day if that should be his fate. All his training and all his instincts were engaged. He watched the man move as he followed him, measured his stride, and felt the weight of him in the crushed undergrowth around the trees. It was a short stride for a man of such size and bulk. The way he moved suggested total reliance on brute force, ponderous, without finesse, and not very agile for a renowned knife fighter.

Michael had shed his MP5 to make this pursuit, but he retained his Glock. Three times he sighted it on his opponent's back, but the trees, brush, and uneven terrain interfered with a clean shot. It had to be clean, or he could lose him. It was hard enough to keep up with him and the terrain grew no easier. He could not stop to get a decent shot, so as the distance widened, he elected to shoot at the run, clean or not, before he should lose him entirely.

The shot struck his opponent in the upper right side of his back. Komodo spun with a bellow, firing the AK wildly, emptying a magazine into the forest and at Michael, hitting him with two rounds, both squarely stopped by his body armor, but the impacts knocked the wind out of him and spun him against a tree. The Glock went flying into the brush.

Michael put his hand on his knife in time to meet Komodo coming in low and pointing up, the hardest approach to counter. He used a leg to block the attack, feeling a slice along his calf as Komodo brought him down with a sweep against the cut leg. He landed and rolled away just as the Yakut knife plunged into the sand beside him. He grabbed the wrist that held it.

His enemy was now bleeding profusely from the gunshot wound and breathing heavily but his strength remained gargantuan. Evidently, brute strength made up a lot for a lack of agility. They did not wrestle. Michael held that wrist and by twisting, jumping, dropping, and rolling, avoided the giant's arms and legs as Komodo telegraphed each attempt to hit him, landing one ineffectual glancing fist on Michael's right kidney and then a more serious body blow to the diaphragm.

As he struggled to breathe again, Michael kept hold of the wrist and remembered the training he had practiced the night before. His breath came back with a gasp, and he braced one foot against a tree trunk to gain purchase, then used Komodo's furious thrashing as leverage to bring himself to a stand.

The dragon stabbed the air within millimeters of his neck as Michael stepped behind him, bringing the man's arm with him. He exposed the underside of the wrist behind his back, brought his knife across it, and watched as his enemy's knife dropped into the pine needles.

Michael finished him more mercifully than Komodo had ever done to a victim. He found his Glock, retrieved the MP5, and limped to the safehouse.

# TWENTY-ONE

Misha ran point. It was not the necessity of what he was doing that irked him most, though it did. It always did. He was in a more or less permanent state of irk much of the time and wondered what Alex would think of the observation or his use of the English word. It irked him more than usual this time because she was not safe at home. She was in harm's way. No matter what he did, no matter what he said, the bloody woman insisted on worrying about the future. Damn it. *You do not have a future if you do not stay alive now.* He tried to tell her. He argued. The more they fought, the more he wanted her.

He shifted his thoughts in a long-practiced direction. The back of the target sentry loomed before him. The man did not hear him, would never hear him, would never hear anything again, and the others in the building would never hear him die. All of it irked Misha.

He gave the signal to the team behind him. Steve handed him an MP5 submachine gun as he passed into the building. Sergei nodded to him. Mara followed Steve. The gunfire began immediately. They had only four fighters left to defeat, now that the sentry was dead, then five more important targets. The knife fighter was Michael's. Nick was Steve's, and Mara had been assigned to the GRU man. Misha would take out David as he had Sally. She had done her damage by causing the operation and endangering the child. She could not be considered an innocent. Poor, silly, dangerous woman.

Sergei was assigned to take care of Linda because he had recruited her when he was KGB. Misha found that thought more tolerable than the thought of him touching his daughter. The damage these asshole bureaucrats can do, thought Misha. Like Sally, they are too often oblivious to consequences. Sergei had been one of them, in fact had been part of the operation to kill Misha's childhood friend Vasily. Now he did all his damage with a gun. This, at least, Misha understood.

Guns were not as insidious. When you kill with a gun, you know you are guilty of something heinous. No such awareness accompanies a pen.

Mara inhabited a special category in Misha's worldview. Sergei had better remember that.

He helped the others clear the building, saw the GRU babysitter exit through a side door, and saw Mara run after her quarry. He knew Michael and Mara were more than adequate for the task ahead of them, but this son-in-law of his? A former babysitter like Steve, but for the other side. Sometimes too much like Steve.

There were no signs of the other three targets, so where were they?

He stood at the building entrance with Sergei. The flies had become thick on the sentry's body, buzzing a grizzly din in the decaying space. He watched his son-in-law shiver at the sight. Good, he thought, let him remember this should he ever think to hurt Mara.

Misha turned on his heel and headed for the safehouse, leaving Sergei to follow. He did not like this silence. He hated not knowing what was going on at the house. Was the bloody woman obeying him for once and staying inside? Was she wearing her SIG? Was she still alive? His pace quickened with this thought, even before the call in their ears from Skosh. At that call, he broke into a run.

# TWENTY-TWO

It took Mara and the others less than two minutes to clear the building and account for all four fighters, most of them half naked in the sweltering heat and still hungover. Komodo ran out the back. There was no sign of any of the other four main targets until Misha caught a glimpse of a closing side door leading to the outside. He signaled to Sergei who was closest and who opened it carefully to see the retreating back of Gennady, the GRU babysitter.

"I will …," he began.

"No," said Mara. "We have a plan." She was already running when she reached the door.

Gennady was not headed to Charlemagne's safehouse. His direction meant his destination must be David's safehouse. Mara acted quickly on intuition. A car driven by one of Jay's watchers was parked at the end of the block. She switched her radio out of network and into main.

"Jay," she said. There was an agonizing pause before Skosh answered. "Get Jay," she said. She came level with the car. The driver stared straight ahead watching the retreating back of a man in a suit, but did nothing. Mara knew Gennady did not fit any of the descriptions that had been given out and appeared unarmed. Plus, he was leaving, not trying to get into the area. The car windows were open. It was already eighty-three degrees Fahrenheit under the trees and humid, hotter in the car. Mara reached in, unlocked the passenger door, and sat down, pointing her Glock at the unlucky watcher.

"Hands on the wheel," she said. "Drive."

"What…?

"Straight ahead."

"Jay here," said a voice in her ear.

"I need you to call your guy." She looked at her driver. "What's your name?"

He seemed to have no answer, so she put a round past his nose and out his window.

"Connolly," he said.

"Connolly," she told Jay. "Call him and tell him to do as I say."

"I need to be sure."

"Yes, it's her," came through the radio, blasted by both Sergei and Steve, the latter with an epithet.

Jay called Connelly on another channel, provided authentication, and ordered compliance. Connolly followed Mara's instructions to the letter. Gennady had parked a nondescript rental car on the street a few yards before the driveway leading to David's safehouse. As he pulled away from the curb, Mara told Connolly to follow him.

"Are you local to this area? Do you live here?" she asked after a few minutes.

"Yes."

"Where do you think he is going? This is not the way to his hotel."

"Um. Maybe the beach. On the island."

"Island?"

"Okaloosa Island. There's a popular beach there. Yes, I'd say he's headed for the bridge."

"Is it populated? Are there many people?"

"Yes. Especially with this heat."

Mara laid her Škorpion machine pistol and Glock on the floor and took off her vest, her t-shirt, then her armor, belt, boots, trousers, and socks.

"What are you doing?" asked Connolly.

She had to take the wire out of her ear. She would be on her own. She debated whether to give it to Connolly to monitor but decided if this took longer than a minute and he answered her radio, it could cost him his life, not by the enemy, but by her team. Neither her husband nor her brother would wait for explanations. Mercy prevailed and she dropped the earpiece and wire into a pocket of the vest on the floor. She fished out the black t-shirt and put it back on, then rummaged for her Glock and a suppressor, checked again that the magazine was full and a round chambered, fitted the suppressor, and shook out her blonde hair saying, "There is his car. Park near it."

As soon as he had parked, she demanded he give her his shirt, covered the Glock with it, and stepped out barefoot onto the hot pavement. "Wait here," she said through the open window.

She looked like any other young woman at the beach. A particularly attractive young woman. She heard wolf whistles.

It took her a full three minutes to locate her quarry and position herself ahead of him on the crowded beach. Gennady had shed his coat and tie, shoes and socks, and had opened his shirt to the Gulf breeze as he walked along the wet sand. She approached, smiling.

He smiled back.

She said hi as she walked up to him. He said hi back, too busy looking at her to remark on the shirt she had pressed to his chest. He fell face forward into the water. Mara acted shocked and ran through the crowd screaming "Help him!" She made her exit to the parking lot as the crowd surged toward the dead man.

Even as Connolly wondered if he should call Jay—it had been almost four minutes—she slid into the seat next to him band told him to drive to the safehouse, our safehouse she clarified, the one where Turner was.

Everyone was outside when she arrived, and Sergei was on the ground. So was her mother. Sergei was bleeding and swearing while Steve applied a tourniquet to his leg. Her mother lay on her back, very still. Theresa held her wrist and pulled up an eyelid.

Mara did not notice the burning heat of the pavement on the soles of her feet as she ran to Misha.

## TWENTY-THREE

Steve Donovan's target was a no-show. Michael and Mara had followed theirs and Sergei knew where to find his, but Nick never came near the teams or the remnants of teams Charlemagne had just taken care of. Who would behave like that? Steve asked himself. He knew the answer immediately because he had been one, briefly, unsuccessfully, but he knew a babysitter by smell if nothing else. The GRU guy was a babysitter for the tattoo guy. So who was Nick supposed to be babysitting? Not the collection of drunken louts they had just massacred. Who then? David. Nick was grooming a computer nerd to become a specialist. Steve couldn't help snorting. Then he remembered Mara was a computer nerd and also a highly effective specialist.

Back to the business at hand, he told himself. Because he's a babysitter, Nick will wait it out somewhere. Where? At David's safehouse. All of this thinking took no more than a few seconds. He eased his MP5 off the sorest part of his shoulder and set off at an easy jog. Sally had exhausted Misha's patience, finally. He didn't know how he felt about it. Relief mixed with pain mixed with, he had to admit, some joy. He had his son again. He remembered himself at eleven and shuddered. Misha was right. Sally had to go. How many deaths was she responsible for now? He couldn't count them. He could only count the ones so far on this trip, the ones he had taken care of, the one he was about to, all of them bad guys, but they would not have crossed paths this time out but for Sally's big mouth. And that didn't include any additional information she may have blabbed that could lead these bozos home to Vasily's Carpet.

Shit. Eleven years old.

Steve waited for what looked like one of Jay's watchers to pull away from the curb down from the entrance to David's safehouse, then crept around a high bordering hedge. Two cars were parked side by side in front of the door. One had an occupant in the driver's seat.

He walked up, in full armor, tactical vest festooned with magazines, radio, knife, and holster. The holster was empty because his Beretta was in his hand. He looked at the man reading a Russian magazine. It looked from the side like pictures of Nick he had seen, but he had to be sure. Misha was not keen on mistakes. Steve was not keen on Misha's reactions to mistakes. He tapped on the window.

"Hey, tovarishch," he said.

Nick Beridze turned and saw the muzzle of the suppressor, but had no time to react.

Steve walked back to the team's safehouse and found a disaster underway in front of it.

## TWENTY-FOUR

Sergei cleared a nest of two vory in one room, still groggy, barely dressed, and meters from their weapons. He let them get a step closer to their guns before he let them have it. Misha would not approve. Misha did not approve of much. He certainly did not approve of Sergei, though he was more restrained in his disapproval than Mikhail, that is, Michael. He must get used to these Western names.

The root cause of all this disapproval was, of course, Mara. They pictured her as an innocent maiden. Sergei knew her to be all woman, young, yes, innocent in some ways perhaps, but not the blushing bride they thought she was. He smiled to himself as he trudged through the countless rooms in this decayed palace of capitalism. He had been her first, and as long as he had any say in it, would remain her only. But she never blushed.

Sergei cleared room after room, quickly, and efficiently, and met up again with his father-in-law back at the entrance, where Misha's earlier fly-covered work lay staring at the ceiling in a surprisingly large pool of coagulating blood. Sergei could not help a grimace. Misha's ice blue stare seemed like a challenge, as in, *say something so that I may answer you*. Sergei had no desire for one of Misha's answers. The man was always gentler to him than he was to Steve, if anything about Misha could be described as gentle, but that was purely for Mara's sake. Sergei knew better than to take it as a sign of approval.

"They are not here," he said.

Misha raised an eyebrow at this obvious statement.

"Where could they be?" Sergei asked.

His father-in-law did not answer but began walking back toward the safehouse. Sergei understood instinctively, because of how he felt about

Mara, that Misha had to check on Alex. He wished he could convey this understanding, this empathy, to the iceberg that was Mara's biological father, but they still were not beyond bare tolerance in the relationship. He followed.

They had walked halfway to the house when Skosh's voice broke into the network and their ears.

"There is a problem."

They both began running. As they neared the house, Misha sent Sergei to the left with a hand signal and veered off to the right. They approached using what cover they could find on either side of the property. Sergei stopped behind a large juniper bush planted in front of the neighboring house.

Theresa was outside talking to David. They were about twenty-five feet apart. Who the hell let her out? What the fuck was Skosh thinking? Sergei was going to have a piece of his hide when this was over. Shit. Alex was behind Theresa, but also outside, trying to get her to come back in. Double shit. He did not dare look at Misha's expression. Some things just hold more horror than is necessary in an already overexciting life.

Then he saw Linda. She was walking up with studied nonchalance from behind a car parked on the street, approaching the little scene taking place in front of the safehouse. He knew he had a fresh magazine in his MP5. He silently put his Makarov away and took the MP5 off his shoulder pointing it in her direction. The hand that was toward him was empty, but he could not see the other hand and that bothered him. He watched her attitude. It seemed relaxed, almost friendly. Then he saw just the barest triangle of the bottom corner of an AK-47 stock.

In the next fraction of a second, two people died and three were wounded, one of them critically.

Sergei fired.

Linda screamed, "You bitch!" and at the same instant, brought up her AK to add punctuation.

Alex screamed, "No!" and moved slightly in front of Theresa, her arm stretched out and the sights of her SIG on David.

Theresa stood frozen as she watched David's arm come up, a semi-automatic pistol in his hand, on its way to aim at her head.

Misha fired and killed David.

Sergei's burst from the MP5 interrupted Linda's, but as she died, three rounds escaped the aborted fire from the AK. The first hit Alex and she went down. The second hit Justin in the window where he had placed a speaker and played the tape of Linda confessing to the plan to kill her husband. It was the last thing David heard. The third bullet hit Sergei, causing a lot of bleeding from his thigh and bringing him down. He told himself it was not spurting and therefore not the artery, but he did not like the way it gushed.

He may have lost consciousness. He wasn't sure. The next thing he knew, Steve was applying a tourniquet and Theresa was gently slapping Alex's cheek. And the look on Misha's face was just too terrible to stay conscious of. Sergei allowed himself to pass out again.

## TWENTY-FIVE

Skosh and the other babysitters—let's face it, he thought, even Jay understands he is essentially babysitting a gaggle of killers, so he can get off his lawman high horse even if he won't admit it out loud. Jay's shadow, young and over-educated Justin, didn't have the foggiest idea why he was there or what he was doing, but that didn't mean he wasn't babysitting. Once these thoughts had settled in Skosh's brain and he felt justified in calling the FBI guys fellow babysitters—even though he knew Frank would balk at that, being strictly old school—but once that was settled, he turned his attention to their common problems, namely Theresa and Alex. Two of the most powerful men he knew, two men whose word was absolute among their subordinates, Mack and Frank, could not fully control these women. And now he and the others were responsible for their safety.

Skosh put himself in charge. Frank had more experience but was retired and worried about his daughter. Jay was active and experienced but busy with the army of watchers he controlled. Also, Jay was the best shot, though Skosh suspected he and Frank could compete. He wasn't sure about Alex. The only thing he knew about Alex was that she was their most precious charge, despite Theresa being family, because nobody would want to face Mack if anything happened to her.

Everybody climbed to the front bedroom at his insistence to await news. Skosh brought the radio receiver from the conference room, even though they were all wired. He would have been happy with just having a lookout up here, but he did not want the two women unsupervised for even a moment.

The six of them had been up there for almost half an hour when Jay answered a call from Mara. They spent another ten minutes taking turns peering through the blinds to the front yard when they heard a voice outside.

"It's Bertram," said Jay.

They heard him shouting through the glass.

"Theresa! Theresa, I know you're there. I just want to talk to you. I think I have a right to some answers. I won't hurt you. I would never hurt you. See? I'm not armed."

"His hands are clear," said Jay.

"I should talk to him," said Theresa.

"No!" Skosh was gratified that even Alex joined this chorus.

"Wait a minute," said Justin, checking outside. "I know that guy. We were in a couple of classes together at MIT. He's an asshole. Worst kind of mama's boy. A mean coward."

"No shit?" said Skosh through clenched teeth. "Tell us more—some other time!"

"I can't see behind him," said Jay on the other side of the window. "Just because his hands are clear doesn't mean he's not armed. Also, there could be others out there. Too many bushes on both sides. Who set up this safehouse anyway?" He gave an accusing glance at Justin, who shrugged back at him.

"Well, I need the bathroom," said Theresa. "I'll be right back."

Alex seemed uneasy. "I'll just stay with her." She left the room and, in another moment, she was shouting from the stairs.

Justin would have followed them all down the stairs, but Skosh told him to cover David from the window.

"Fire if he shows a weapon," said Skosh. "Don't wait."

"I can't," shouted Justin before Skosh was halfway down. "She's in the way." He knew he was not a good enough shot with Theresa blocking the path of any rounds he might throw at David. Rather than stay upstairs pointlessly, he ran down the steps after Skosh with an idea. Remembering Alex had told him to cue the tape of Linda saying she planned the death of her husband, he pressed play in the conference room and grabbed the speaker, unspooling the wire as he ran to the front room window and opened it.

Frank screamed at his daughter to get back inside. Jay ran back upstairs in a futile quest to find any angle of sight on David that was not blocked by Theresa and now by Alex. Skosh broke into the team frequency and with all the urgency he could put into his voice and the greatest understatement he could find words for, he said, "Skosh here. We have a problem."

Maybe the tape made David pause just long enough for Sergei and Mack to reach the house. Skosh slid down the stairs and into a horror scene. The front door was open. Theresa stood, tall, majestic, and frozen, her great mane of dark auburn hair hanging in waves around her shoulders. Linda's voice came from a speaker held by Justin at the open window. David held a Makarov pointed at Theresa's head from no more than fifteen feet away. Alex stood in a side stance, her right arm extended and her finger on the trigger of her SIG Sauer.

Into this tense scene, Linda came out of nowhere brandishing an AK-47 and screaming, "You bitch!" Though which woman she was referring to, Skosh couldn't say. At the same moment, Justin flew backward into the living room wall, Linda fell amid a burst of automatic fire coming out of a juniper bush, David's head exploded and he fell, and Alex crumpled to the ground.

Theresa turned to her immediately and searched for a pulse. Mack ran up and looked down at the two women, his own SIG still in his hand at his side. David and Linda were dead.

Frank ran to Theresa carrying a bag of medical supplies. "What else do you need?"

"I need her to live," said Theresa through tears. "Come on Alex. Her breathing is not right. Get the damned vest off her. Quick! I need to see."

It was Mack who holstered his gun and knelt to take the armor off his wife. At first, they could not see the bullet hole. Then as Theresa gently compressed the chest, blood and air seeped and hissed from a small hole in Alex's side. There was surprisingly little blood, but Alex lay unconscious.

Theresa checked her pupils. There was no response. "Come on, please, Alex. I'm so sorry. I'm such a fool. Please forgive me. I'll marry him. I will. Just live, Alex, just live for me. I'll need you!"

She checked again. "The pulse is good," she said with a sigh "But I think the lung has collapsed and I'm sure there's a head wound. We have to get her to a hospital."

Alex shuddered through a hissing breath but did not regain consciousness.

"No," said Mack, standing up.

She stared, incredulous.

"Papa," said Charlie, "Steve and I will take care of the other matter and meet you at the airplane."

Mack nodded. Theresa stared at Charlie now. He was drenched in blood and had some active seepage coming from one leg.

"Frank," said Charlie, "load the car when Steve gets here with it. Jay, some of your people can help, but only the locked trunks. Frank, you check every trunk and watch their hands. Jay, when will the ambulances be here?"

"In about half a minute. I called them from the kitchen. Goodwin was hit, but the vest stopped it. He can help."

"She will die without proper attention!" said Theresa, tears streaming down her face.

"Then you will give her that attention," said Mack.

"I can't do it alone and without equipment and my best helper is the patient. Where is Sergei?"

"He needs you as well."

Mara ran up to Mack and buried her head on his chest, sobbing. Mack had no idea what to do. Mara had always treated him as the not-exactly evil but certainly suspect stepfather, though he was her biological father as well. He carefully patted her back, whispered something to her, and she turned to Theresa.

"You must save her. Please save her."

"As I just tried to explain to your father ..." Theresa began her litany of impossibilities, but neither Mack nor Mara was listening. For the first time, Mara did not correct the word father to stepfather. The significance was not lost on either of them.

"Listen to me, Theresa," said Mack. "These men will help you." He pointed to several EMTs walking up from two discreet ambulances. "You will get her ready to fly. Also Sergei," he turned to Jay. "Goodwin?"

"Last priority."

Theresa sobbed.

"Because he's not that badly hurt, Theresa," said Jay. "Concentrate on Alex. Here comes Donovan with the car."

A black Mercedes pulled into the driveway and Frank began supervising as the watchers loaded the trunk, then he and Skosh carried in the open bags. Charlie climbed into the passenger seat. Skosh handed him a wet rag to wipe his face and the car pulled out.

She did not know how she did it, but Theresa managed to check everything on both patients as they were loaded into the ambulances. Mara and Frank rode with Sergei. Mack joined Theresa in the ambulance with the unconscious Alex.

"I don't understand why you refuse to take her to a hospital," she said. "She's unconscious too long and I don't know why, and there's a chest wound. She needs …"

"She would be in more danger there. We are, all of us, in danger. Your father will explain more fully later. We must leave now. There is no succor for us in this country. It is a country of laws, but also very open and very armed. All three things are dangerous. The law is powerful and can be used against us by those who manipulate it. We cannot always hide in such openness, and all weapons are easily available to our enemies without remark. They would not miss such an opportunity. No bullet is reversed by law."

"But if you're leaving, how can I help her?"

"The airplane is equipped. You will have everything you need. And Mara will help. She is also an accomplished nurse." He looked at her with his brow furrowed. "Did you not understand you are coming with us?"

## TWENTY-SIX

There was one happy person on the airplane. Danny could not believe the luxury of being in a large private jet, and he reveled in the squalor of unshaven men, filthy and stinking and exhausted. There were a couple of women, he noted, but everybody else was a guy like him, not a bunch of girls, and no Linda. These guys weren't evil in his book, no matter what Mom said. He knew they had rescued him, but he wasn't sure it would be okay to say so. Maybe they wouldn't believe him, either. He had made a plan to escape, but this was better. After all, he was just a kid. He hadn't even worked out where he would go.

All in all, he couldn't be happier.

Steve could not help glancing at his son. He wanted to stare but knew it would make the kid uncomfortable. The last time he had seen him, Danny was a toddler. There had been no pictures, no word, though he knew Misha kept a close eye on the boy and his mother to keep her from jeopardizing his safety. He could not believe Danny was sitting across from him now, firing off questions about airplanes. Sally had not told him that his dad had been a fighter pilot. She did tell him that his dad and his friends were evil men.

Danny's next questions were about the guns everybody wore. David took him shooting once, he said, but his mom had forbidden him to do that again. He asked shyly if Steve would take him out to the range sometime. It was this question that brought home to Steve the magnitude of the change he was making in his son's life. It made him pause, not with a bunch of philosophical considerations, for he was never a philosophical man. He paused with the practical implications. He questioned his ability to guide the boy through this change without damage. Steve's vocation, such as it was, had been forced on him. He wasn't sorry about what he was and flattered himself that he was grounded in his own grim reality, but he wanted any such decision to be Danny's alone, not forced by circumstance.

"Listen, Danny," he said, "I'm super, super tired and I'll probably fall asleep the minute we're out of US airspace, so I need to make sure you know a few things. You see that man over there?" He pointed at Frank.

"You mean the one who looks kinda like a frog?"

"The very one. If you need anything or have any questions, you ask him, okay? If he's asleep you can wake him up, but under no circumstances should you wake up anybody else. Even me. It'll probably get boring because it's a long flight. It might be a good idea to get some sleep yourself. But whatever you do, don't wake up anybody except him. His name is Frank."

Steve worried until they were half a nautical mile out of US airspace, when he fell into an instant deep sleep.

Frank had no concerns about what airspace they were in and so had been asleep since takeoff. It was a troubled sleep, with nightmares about Theresa being wed to a monster who never turned into a handsome prince. He felt cheated of a fairy tale ending to her story every time she repeated 'I do.'

Sergei was in considerable pain. Theresa had disinfected, sutured, bandaged, and medicated for infection but could not do anything about the pain yet. Mara helped her with both him and Alex, who was still unconscious. He envied her that sweet oblivion. Not long before he was due to get the blessed shot, Theresa and Misha got into it and the repercussions fell upon him. As junior man on the team, it was to be expected, and Misha did practically carry him into the main cabin himself and then authorized the morphine fifteen minutes early, but... Sergei was asleep before he could finish the thought.

Michael wondered what it would be like to have a wife. As he watched his father unravel, he wondered if he wanted one. Misha had not grieved like this over Michael's mother, over his sister's death, yes, but even that was different from this, and Alex was still alive right now. Did he want to care that much? He once thought he was in love but the woman betrayed him and tried to kill him. That eradicated any grief he might have felt for her. Given his circumstances, did he need such an additional level of anxiety as his father was showing? Alex seemed to think so, which is why she had come and why she now appeared to be on the brink of death. He wanted Theresa, but did he want her that badly? She still had not answered him. What if she said no? With that thought, when he answered this question truthfully, he reached a first true understanding of the devastation his father was facing.

Mara helped Theresa examine and treat the damage to her mother's poor chest and back. The bullet had gone in under her arm and through the side gap in her soft body armor as she held her SIG with a single straight arm, sighting it on David's head. It had ripped through the lung, exited, and embedded itself on the inside of the vest at the back. It was not a hollow point, for some strange reason, which gave them hope.

Sergei also owed his life to this detail. The damage to his thigh was painful, but the bullet had traveled straight through, missing the artery, saving him the agony of surgical removal and not creating massive damage on the way out.

Now that they were out of the airspace, all Mara wanted to do was sleep. She was the one who suggested they move Sergei so Misha could sleep in the cot next to Alex, thus ending a conflict of egos between surgeon and specialist that was becoming increasingly heated. Misha demanded more and more detailed explanations from an exasperated and imperious Theresa. Sergei complained about moving, loudly and unreasonably, but he was in pain after all, and she would make it up to him when he was well enough.

Theresa was delighted with the cramped but well-equipped medical room on the airplane. She had everything she needed except a modern way to investigate the interior of a body without cutting it open. In this case, that did not matter as much with the bullet wounds. She would have to cut, trace, and repair tissues in the path the bullet had taken through Alex's ribcage anyway. Alex was still unconscious.

She found Mara every bit as skilled a helper as Alex had been with Steve's injury.

The continued unconsciousness was her main concern. There was a hefty hematoma at the rear of the occipital on the right side that Theresa checked carefully for signs of fracture, but without an x-ray, she could not be sure it was completely clear, and anyway, there was almost certainly a severe concussion. She worried about internal bleeding, but the signs indicated all was as well as could be expected.

All, except for the large, intrusive, frantic irritation that was Alex's husband. He seemed to think he could cure her by sheer force of will and minute, critical supervision of the attending surgeon. He was in the way. When he was not in the way, he was in the process of putting himself in the way. Between directing Mara and tending to her patient, Theresa anticipated his movements and headed him off strategically so that their interaction became a constant bumbling dance of two incompatible bodies intent upon occupying the same cramped space in an airplane at altitude.

Mara's suggestion that Sergei move out of the surgery and into the cabin so that Misha could lie down seemed the perfect solution. Even so, Theresa had to put her foot down and even shout at him to stay in his cot. She offered him a sedative. He glowered at her.

"Please, Mama," said Mara, well within his hearing, "wake up before he drives us all mad."

He glowered at her, too.

Misha had been quiet for half an hour when Frank came back to check on his daughter and urge her to rest.

"I'll sit here with Alex and come get you if anything changes. Go. Sleep."

Theresa went to the main cabin where she found Michael still awake. She sat down next to him and he put his arm around her. She fell asleep on his shoulder.

## TWENTY-SEVEN

Having evicted his daughter to the main cabin, Frank took her seat at the side of the gurney where Alex lay as if asleep, unconscious but breathing. A machine on the other side of the bed automatically monitored and displayed her vital signs. To Frank's left, a drop-down cot held Mack, his arm shielding his eyes. Frank doubted he was asleep. He knew he wouldn't be if it were Maryann lying here. But it didn't matter. He had to have his say.

"Alex," He took and held her limp hand. "Frank here. I know—we all know—you came out because of Theresa. I suspect your reason was Charlie. I suppose I should start calling him Michael." He paused at this unwelcome thought, swallowed the acid it caused, and continued. "Because they don't know you, the others—I'm talking about the non-team members—don't understand why it was so important. I want you to know that I know why."

He took a deep breath and hung his head for a moment. Too many uses of the word 'know,' but it was unavoidable. "I know why and I approve. I will do my best to be happy for them."

He choked a bit.

"If Theresa can do half for Char… Michael what you've done for Mack, she will have lived a worthy life. I can't stand in the way of that. You are also not finished with Mack, by the way, so you can't chalk it all up to one good deed. They still need you and now Theresa needs you, so I'm begging you to come around. I'm praying you can hear me and are fighting to come to the surface."

Frank's breath caught. "Can you do that again or did I imagine it?" A pause, and then a whisper. "I did feel it. You heard me."

They grappled briefly in the narrow space between the bed and the cot as Mack pulled Frank from the chair and shoved him toward the door.

It took a few minutes for Frank to wake Theresa without waking the filthy, bloody specialist with his arm around her. Son-in-law, he practiced saying to himself. He went back to the medical room with her, though she insisted it wasn't necessary. He was very glad he did.

Alex was awake, groggy, smiling, and drifting off again. Her hand rested on the blond head of her husband. He sat in the chair next to her, sound asleep with his head on the gurney, an arm stretched across her stomach, the other around her head.

As Theresa raised her hand to wake Mack, Frank whispered "No," and Alex shook her head.

"But he looks so uncomfortable," she said.

"I'll explain later," said Frank. "I'll explain a lot of things."

...

They landed after midnight. Theresa had an impression of a huge house, a mansion, really, and then a cavernous lower-level hallway, gorgeously carpeted down its long length, with doors on either side. It was here that she found her mother and held her for what seemed like her whole life but lasted no more than a few seconds. Her mother was equally unwilling to let go, but the bustle of the returning team, their gear, the stretcher bearing Alex, and the boy watching with sleepy wide eyes as lockers and weapons made their way through various doorways brought them to an awareness of their separate responsibilities.

It took another two hours of jumping at noises, disinfecting cuts and scrapes, suturing

Michael's leg, and arguing with Misha about how to care for Alex before Theresa was allowed to collapse on a bed in a room she only dimly perceived. She woke before dawn and turned on a bedside lamp to investigate the weight in the bed next to her. Michael lay there, profoundly asleep. He was clean—ish, she decided. As she gazed at him half in and half out of the covers, she realized it was the first time she had ever seen him without a gun within easy reach.

On her way back from the toilet, she noticed his Glock and holster lying on an ornamental table against one wall. She stepped toward it and was about to reach her hand out curiously.

"Don't." In the dim light and silence, the single word held a suggestion of menace that brought the realities of the last three days to the forefront of her memory.

"Come back to bed."

"Are you ordering me?"

"I am strongly suggesting."

"Why?"

"It seems your father has not told you what you need to know to stay safe with us. Therefore, I must do so. Come here."

The last strong suggestion was an order, she decided, and she was tempted to ignore it until the word 'safe' triggered a mental image of her father stopping her hand from touching a sleeping Misha in the airplane and promising to explain later. It was followed by an intense feeling of shame that she had allowed herself to be so thoroughly hoodwinked into leaving the safehouse to talk to David despite all the evidence she had of the danger. Really, she thought, I was no better than Sally in that moment.

After an interlude that revealed the real reason for his order and reminded her why she had accepted him, they exchanged some home truths. His dealt with the dangers of behaving surreptitiously around him and the others, hers with the inadvisability of ordering her around.

It was not yet dawn when he slipped out to his room, taking the holster and its contents with him, and citing servants as the reason. She suspected that their fathers were the more likely cause.

Michael's instruction paid off in the next fifteen minutes when Theresa walked into Alex's room, where a hospital bed had been thrown up at the foot of a large four-poster. She wanted to check on her but found Misha asleep in the same bed as the patient so crept out and closed the door behind her.

"You'd be better off making a bit of noise," said a loud voice on her right. "And keep it cheerful. Never be furtive. It's like an alarm call."

"Dad!"

The door behind her opened. Misha stood scowling at Theresa's father.

"We are not specimens in a zoo, Frank."

"Nonetheless, I see your SIG is in your hand."

Theresa looked at the hand down at Misha's side. It was, indeed, holding his pistol. She moved to step away but was blocked by his other arm.

"What did you want?"

"I came to check on Alex."

Misha stepped to one side, opened the door wide, and beckoned her into the room with a lift of his chin.

"Frank," he said as her father began to walk away, "ask Maryann to please come here. I must speak with her."


# TWENTY-EIGHT

The patient smiled. The irritating appendage that was her husband did not. Father-in-law, Theresa reminded herself. He reholstered his weapon and laid both back down on a nearby dresser. Would she ever get used to this? She concentrated on the patient, starting with vital signs, when her mother knocked and was admitted.

Apart from last night's brief hug, they had not seen each other in a year but managed to keep to only another quick embrace before the disheveled, unshaven, scowling man wearing an exquisite brocade dressing gown cleared his throat pointedly and spoke to her mother.

"I apologize for seeing you when not properly dressed. Will you sit down, please?" He indicated a chair next to a Chippendale table. He spoke English, though Maryann's German was more than competent.

"You know that we have brought Steve's son Danny back with us. After breakfast, Steve and I will meet with him in my study. I must speak with Steve before then but do not want to leave the boy alone. Will you sit with him for fifteen minutes and then bring him to us in my office upstairs?"

"Yes, of course," said Maryann, mystified.

He did not continue. He had become very still, triggering in all three women the memory of danger, until they realized he chose his next words carefully and with hesitation but without a hint of threat. They relaxed.

"If he is normal," said Misha, "Danny will be upset after we have spoken with him. Will you be willing to wait for him upstairs? You might take him then to the kitchen for some biscuits. Encourage him to speak of his mother. Allow him to cry. He will need to cry but will be unwilling to do so in our presence."

Alex closed her eyes and frowned. Theresa opened hers wide. Maryann stared into Misha's.

"Are you saying Sally is dead?"

"Yes. But you must allow us to tell him."

"Did Steve kill her?"

"No."

"That means you did. Did you gut her like a fish?"

Alex winced.

A long, dangerous pause full of electricity stretched out, dominating the room before he replied in a soft menacing purr, "She received more mercy than she deserved. Now, I must dress. Please tell August I require coffee in my dressing room. Immediately."

He took his gun with him and closed the dressing room door softly behind him, no doubt in deference to Alex.

...

Steve gave his son a perfunctory introduction before leaving Maryann to her brief task of watching over the boy. She suggested they sit down in the sitting room of Steve's new three-room suite. The place was comfortable but bare of mementos or decoration. The utilitarian furniture lacked character though a few beautiful antique cabinets, a nice carpet, and well-stuffed chairs covered in soft leather provided sufficient comfort. Nonetheless, to Maryann, the place felt cold and unfriendly.

"How do you like your room, Danny?"

The boy shrugged. "It's good. It's really big."

He has his father's eyes, thought Maryann. And his mother's beauty. As the mother of four sons, she was aware that being a pretty child was not always a good thing for a small boy. She searched for a way to open a conversation, but he started one before she could speak.

"My mom signed papers so I can live with my dad. His boss told me so. He had the papers in his coat at the hotel. I didn't bring any clothes. Dad said that's okay, my stuff will be sent here. I had a bath, but these clothes are dirty and I'm going to a meeting. I should have better clothes, don't you think? My dad wore a suit today. Do you think I can get a suit?"

"Eventually, yes of course," said Maryann.

"But I'm going to a meeting this morning." He gave her a worried, almost pleading look.

"Your hair is combed and you don't smell," Maryann said, remembering when her boys were this age.

"That's what my dad said." He nodded with approval at this and looked around the room as if seeing it for the first time. "The men on the airplane all smelled bad. And they all had guns. My mom hates guns, even though her friends all have guns, even Linda. I hate Linda."

"Why?"

"She pretends she likes Mom, but really she hates her. I see how she looks at her sometimes. She hates me, too. The guys all like Mom, but they don't like me either. I bet nobody tells my dad he has eyes like a girl's."

"I bet they don't," said Maryann, truthfully.

"My mom won't let me learn how to fight, like with karate or something. She says it's good to be pretty." He sighed. "It's good for her maybe, but not for me. I hope my dad will let me take karate lessons."

"Is it really bad at your school?" asked Maryann. "I mean the bullies?"

The boy nodded and looked away. "I love my mom," he said after a pause, "but I'm really glad my dad rescued me."

"Rescued you?"

"Yeah. My mom doesn't believe it, but her friends want to kill me. They know I don't like them."

"That doesn't necessarily mean they want to kill you."

He looked her in the eye with a solemnity well beyond his age. "I heard one of them tell her I'm a liability. That was the word he used. I looked it up. He was saying he thinks I'm dangerous."

"What did your mom say?"

"She laughed and called him a tease. He wasn't teasing. I know the difference. He has a gun, too."

Maryann would have to tell Misha. She would have to admit to herself, at least, that he may, just may, have had a reason to kill Sally. He reads minds, she thought with a grimace. He'll know I see the problem. *It's dim to me, but I see it.*

She swallowed this limited portion of crow with all the grace she could muster as she led her charge upstairs to Misha's office.

## TWENTY-NINE

"You're going to send him to Colorado? I just got him and he's going to leave?" Steve's words did not hide the note of belligerence he tried so hard to conceal.

"I did not say that," said Misha. He lifted a silver pot from a tray atop a small, ornamented table and poured coffee into two bone china cups with saucers. "I said we must give him a choice." He handed one cup to Steve.

Steve took the cup and stared at the empty fireplace before them. It was summer and thus no fire, but he wanted one. He wanted dancing flames and warmth and safety. He saw only cold stone and sinking disappointment.

"If we tell him, he will choose his grandparents."

Misha took a long sip of his coffee before answering.

"I think he will stay. He was not happy with his mother."

"How do you know that? And there's a big difference between being unhappy with mom and knowing dad… does what he does." Steve mumbled the last few words into his coffee cup.

"You mean to say he will not want to live in the house of the man who killed his mother."

*Damned mind reader.*

"Steve, he must not begin adolescence without knowing the truth."

"He never has to know. Can't we arrange a story?"

"No fiction will hold indefinitely. He is at the best age now to learn the truth without additional damage. He must know both the facts and the reasons before he makes his decision. Any later and he will feel betrayed. And he will have access to you. Think, Steve, what it would do to him if someday he took vengeance on the father who lied to him?"

The ultimate argument. If you love him, be willing to give him up. Steve's heart sank to his socks. He stared at his cooling coffee. "But why does he have to make a decision? He'll go to Colorado."

"I think not. He does not know his grandparents and is sufficiently intelligent to understand he will be as badly bullied in any school he attends there."

Steve's head came up with a jerk. He stared at Misha. "Bullied? Why do you say that?"

"Because he looks like you, except he is even more beautiful. His mother was not likely to understand, let alone take action. I think his life in North Carolina was difficult at best. He will not want to repeat that experience in Colorado."

Steve had never told Misha about his childhood. He sighed. "How do I tell him?"

"I will tell him. I will explain that you did not kill her."

Steve snorted and said in English, "Near as makes no difference."

Misha took a moment to process this adage and replied, "He will be interested only in who pulled the trigger. You may, and should, answer any subsequent questions about your agreement when, and if, they are posed. Boys are very literal."

They both had been boys once upon a time and bowed to the truth of this. A soft knock at the door interrupted them. It opened to admit Danny while Maryann indicated she wished to speak to Misha.

Danny was sipping a soda when Misha took his seat and introduced himself properly.

"Tell me about the man who said you are a liability," he said.

Steve's eyes widened involuntarily. He turned his head hoping his son had not seen his surprise.

Danny launched into a description of all his mother's friends. The liability man, as he called him, came at night when he was supposed to be asleep, but unlike Nick, he didn't come to kiss his mom. He came to lecture her about code books and stuff like he was James Bond or something, but he was too tall and scrawny with a beaky nose.

"How many times were you awake when he came?" asked Misha.

"Every time." In answer to Misha's skeptical look, Danny said, "I kept records. It's all written down. That's how I know he works with Arkady, not for him. He said that a lot."

"Arkady? From the embassy?"

Danny nodded.

"And your records? Where are they?"

Danny gave a detailed description of his hiding place, then described his mother's less secure hiding place for the code books she received from Nick, Arkady, and Liability Man. She never used them. Each man had to go over procedures again with her at least once a month.

Misha rang a service bell and summoned Frank.

"Call Skosh," he said when Frank arrived upstairs, then asked Danny to describe the hiding places once more. When he had gone, Misha turned again to Danny and began the difficult conversation, while Steve held his breath.

"You shot her?" said the boy, with a slight tremor in his voice.

"Yes," said Misha.

"Why?" He was fighting back tears.

"Because she refused to stop putting my team in danger. She also put you in danger."

"I just now told you that," said Danny.

"Yes, but there are others who want to hurt you besides the people you told us about now. You know my friend took a bullet saving your life when you were very young."

Danny nodded. "Dad told me. I'm sorry Louis died last year. I wish I could say thank you."

He looked at Misha with a furrowed brow. "What team is in danger? Do you guys play basketball or something?" Both Misha and his dad seemed very tall to him, and he knew nothing about sports. His mom never allowed him to play anything or even watch it on TV.

"Before I answer you," said Misha, "I must have your answer. Do you intend to stay, or do you prefer to live with your grandparents?"

The boy looked at him frankly. "If I stay, will you promise not to shoot me, too?"

"If you promise not to put anyone in this house in what I decide is a danger."

"If I lived here, then I would be in danger, too, right?"

"Yes."

"And so would The Spare?"

"The Spare?" Misha's brow furrowed.

"Yeah. He wants to be my friend. He's kinda young, but he seems pretty cool. I'm a child of the team, he said, so even though it's not polite to point that out to any of the other kids in the schoolroom upstairs, since we're both children of the team, we should be friends." He paused and said, in a smaller voice, "I've never had a real friend before."

"Other kids? Do you mean children of the staff?"

"Yeah. The Spare explained that."

"Can you describe this 'Spare'?"

"Blond, like you, and he has blue eyes. And he's not Spare. He's 'The Spare'. He told me that's important."

Misha glared at Steve who shook his head. He was sure Danny had not left their rooms.

Turning back to Danny Misha said, "When did you speak to him?"

"This morning. He came to my room." Danny turned to Steve. "You were in the shower. He didn't stay long. But he said I should stay. I don't want to go to Colorado, Dad. I wish Mom wasn't dead, but even if she wasn't, I'd want her to live someplace safe, but I wouldn't go back there. Can I stay with you?"

He turned back to Misha. "I promise not to put anybody in danger."

"Then I promise not to shoot you. Now let us discuss the team and how we do not talk about it."

...

Mack looked perturbed when he handed Danny over to Maryann in the outer office. As she led her charge out through the doorway, she heard him tell his secretary to send for Master Matthias immediately. She wondered briefly what he wanted with the eight-year-old child of a staff member but had no time to think about it further. Danny was so obviously bursting with excitement about his meeting with two of the most dangerous men Maryann had ever had the misfortune to meet, that she found it difficult to bring their conversation around to Sally. They sat on tall stools at an enormous farmhouse table in the kitchen where Cook had laid a plate of cookies and a glass of milk before discreetly leaving them alone.

The boy eventually burst into tears, throwing his arms around her neck, soaking a kitchen towel, and wailing with some vehemence before subsiding into shuddering sniffles. When he said he was ready, she took him upstairs to the schoolroom and left him in the charge of the mathematics tutor.

"What are you doing?" she asked the back of her husband's head when she returned to their room. It was obvious what he was doing. His small suitcase was open on the bed and he was throwing a few clothes in its general direction. She picked up a shirt from the floor and folded it.

"Are we leaving?" she asked, hoping a rift had occurred between Theresa and Michael and the wedding was off. That young man was off the charts dangerous in her books, but she reluctantly reminded herself to trust her daughter's judgment about her future.

"No," said Frank. He threw his shaving bag in the case. Maryann arranged it on one side away from the neatly folded shirt.

"I'm meeting Skosh in North Carolina," he said, "and coming straight back. I should be gone less than two days."

"Are you taking a commercial flight?" She wanted to ask where he would get one. She still had no idea exactly where they were.

He looked at her, his eyes bulging, brows up, and lips suppressing a smile.

"I'm taking the small jet."

"There's a small jet? A second jet?"

"Evidently."

They stared at each other in wonder, then burst out laughing, sharing the memory of decades ago when they invested in a second car, a jalopy that had to be push-started. Frank slammed the case shut. A corner of the shirt stuck out at one side. She opened it, fixed the shirt, and locked it.

She told him about Danny and as an afterthought mentioned the odd summons to an eight-year-old named Matthias, The Spare for short. Leo stared at her when she described the child but said nothing until it was time to leave.

"Whatever you do, Maryann, never mention The Spare to another soul."

After a quick hug, he was gone, without explanation, leaving her to wonder what on earth could be so secret about an eight-year-old boy.

## THIRTY

Frank walked into breakfast on the morning of his daughter's wedding. The household had been informed fifteen minutes before he arrived that the date had changed. He knew about the change before he landed because he brought the reason for it. They were going out again—immediately.

Maryann and Theresa did not know, judging by their smiles. Alex suspected. She gave her husband a narrow gaze, which he was busy ignoring. It delighted Frank to see her up and about. She knew the signs of an impending operation, no doubt, but in this case, the panicking servants should have alerted his wife and daughter that something was up.

They were as cheerful as Mack and Charlie were silent and still. Steve, Sergei, and Mara weren't even there. Packing their gear and cleaning weapons again, no doubt. The bastards were making him break the news.

"Um, Maryann...."

"Hello, Leo. How was your flight?" Her plate was empty. He had come at the end of the meal.

"Fine. Listen, Maryann...."

"We ordered the most beautiful dresses for the wedding, Leo."

A servant put a plateful of eggs and sausages on the table before him. He had lost his appetite. "Are they here already? The dresses, I mean?"

"No, of course not, Dad," said Theresa. "We only ordered them late yesterday."

He looked up at the two blond fucking cowards. They avoided eye contact.

"Maryann listen!" he said with some heat. "You might want to get ready. The wedding's in an hour."

The car took them straight from the chapel to the larger airplane immediately after the ceremony. Alex kissed Misha before solemnly waving goodbye. Maryann handed Frank a freshly packed suitcase. Theresa cried angry tears but kissed her groom passionately.

They spent the flight going over Danny's intelligence contained in the stash Frank brought back from North Carolina.

"We see from Danny's description," said Misha, "that LM is not among those we killed in Florida."

"LM?" asked Frank.

"Liability Man," said Steve. "Danny says he never heard his name."

"Do we know his nationality? Did he have an accent?" asked Mara.

Steve answered again. "He spoke English that sounded normal to Danny, so probably American."

Sergei placed two of Sally's cipher books on the small conference table they were gathered around.

"These are both GRU. Did Danny say who gave them to her?"

"Nick and Arkady, from the embassy," said Steve.

Sergei wrinkled his brow. "Arkady is SVR. I know him. I do not know why he would use a GRU book. But the third book is more interesting. It is not GRU or SVR. It is not even Russian." He passed the book to Misha, who leafed through it and reached behind him to throw it into Frank's lap.

"Stop trying to hide, Frank," Misha said. "We know you are here."

"I don't know why I'm here, and I've never thought it a healthy thing to attend one of your meetings."

"You are here because Skosh needs your instruction when we arrive."

"I'm retired."

"Skosh will benefit from your vast experience. Turner is good but will not be on future operations that take place outside your country."

"And he does not understand the importance of a good car," said Sergei. "Or food."

"In his defense," said Steve, "the Florida safe-house had three working toilets and a decent coffee maker."

There was a general silence in appreciation of the coffee maker.

"And this operation?" asked Frank. "At the risk of making myself conspicuous at one of your meetings, what is the purpose of this little outing?"

Mack's cold glare lasted a moment longer than was comfortable before he answered. "We must find LM. He has threatened Danny. We must know why, who he is, and for whom he is working. There is too much here that we do not know. Ignorance is more deadly than a bullet. Do you not agree?"

"Sometimes knowledge is even more dangerous," he replied, avoiding Mack's considering gaze. He preferred not to meet those eyes, certain the man would read all about The Spare in his own.

Mack allowed a drop of quiet to permeate the cabin, drowning out even the engines. "Then the remedy in such cases," he said, "is silence."

Frank was unsure whether he meant the word as a noun or a verb.

## THIRTY-ONE

Skosh stood on the tarmac next to the Mercedes as the airplane taxied in. He had hoped he'd be allowed more than a week to recover from the Florida op. A lifetime would be optimal, but anything over a week would have been appreciated.

They came down from the airplane looking considerably better than they had climbed aboard a week before. For one thing, they had washed.

Pavlenko still limped but he had combed his hair and shaved, though the wind was undoing any good work the comb had done.

The co-pilot stopped the ground crew from opening the hold. Team members themselves always loaded their gear into the trunk of the Mercedes. There was not as much of it as last time. Skosh crossed his fingers. Maybe they did not expect to stay long.

Frank shook his hand. "Where's Jay?"

"At the safehouse. I managed to get some extra funding, so we got a place where a Mercedes won't stand out. Also, it has a big garage."

"The house is not too big, is it? Big places are a bitch to secure."

Skosh squinted one eye. "Smallest place on the block. That's why it was for rent. Also, I arranged the catering."

"And the coffee?"

"I left that to Jay. Never mess with perfection, I always say. How is Theresa?"

"Married."

"So soon?"

Frank nodded. "This morning."

They walked to the FBO lounge in silence. "They must be worried," said Skosh quietly.

Frank nodded again.

...

For the first time in Frank's memory, there were no complaints.

"You should have picked Skosh over me in the first place," said Steve, referring to his short stint working for Frank.

Sergei stared at the pendant light hanging above him from the two-story vaulted entrance-way ceiling. "Now this is capitalism," he said.

Having been a guest in their house, Frank was not surprised that Mara, Mack, and Charlie were unimpressed with this cheap imitation of opulence. They were more interested in the radios, telephones, alarm system, and two computers arranged conveniently in the usual place—the dining room.

Everybody, Frank included, was interested in dinner. It arrived at the same time as Justin Goodwin, looking wary and carrying his usual toothbrush-sized backpack and a larger case of computer parts. Jay flew him in from Florida.

Jay came out of the kitchen and directed the caterers as soon as the team was out of sight. The food was too delicious for much conversation, leaving a wide opening for Justin to put his foot in it as usual.

"So Frank, how is Theresa?"

Chewing ceased. Even Mack sat back in his chair, knife and fork still poised over his plate, and regarded the young man with a bemused expression.

Charlie's reaction was more pointed. He became very still, which Justin seemed to notice and remember vaguely as not a good thing. Frank had to credit his courage but deplored the foolhardy defiant glare.

"Do you mean my wife?" Charlie said softly in a voice of steel. "She is very well, thank you."

But the young idiot couldn't leave it alone, despite the obvious shut-up stare coming to him from his boss, Jay.

"Oh, congratulations! What is her married name so I can send best wishes to the bride?"

In thirty years, Frank had never heard a name. As far as anybody in his business knew, Mack never had any name. Charlie had used the legend Taylor once, and it was pretty well established that both of them were named some form of Michael, but there had never been the least hint of a last name.

Frank now knew the last name. He learned it that morning in the estate chapel at his daughter's wedding. The name was all over the memorials on the walls and engraved on the slate slabs on the floor. As an intelligence officer and history enthusiast, he had the biggest revelation of his life and could do nothing with it, let alone impart it to the eager young special agent whose less than subtle attempt got him no more than two very cold blue-eyed stares.

Mack turned to Skosh. "We will need you and Jay to follow us to the sovereign house here. We must meet with several people."

"Do you want us to watch the Mercedes again?" asked Jay.

"No. You will come in with us."

"What? No! We'll be blown."

"You are a highly placed FBI official. You are already blown. I need Skosh to look for familiar Russians and for you to recognize any criminals. They have invaded our world." He shook his head at this travesty.

"If I may make a suggestion," said Skosh, carefully avoiding mention of the intersection between crime and intelligence work. "Frank is more suited to this task. Though I would be blown, he is retired. He also knows every Russian ever born in this business, while this side of the world is still very new to me."

Mack nodded slightly and took his time answering. "That was well-spoken and a very plausible argument. I commend you. Frank will stay here and use your attempt as an illustration to teach Mr. Goodwin how to ask questions that will not get him killed. Mara will set up our computer, assuming one of these is ours." He gestured toward the table along one wall. Mara glared at him.

"Nein," he said, addressing the glare.

Frank felt relieved. Tradition ran high in this corner of the special ops world, and testosterone even higher. The wannabe tough guys at the bar would not be a match for her and her entourage, but the babysitters did not need the headaches a dust-up would cause during what he hoped would be a limited operation. Mara could cause a dust-up anytime, anywhere.

Mara's answering protest was brief and shot down with the lift of an eyebrow, but Sergei's stare at Goodwin, who also would be staying behind, took longer and was more disconcerting. It relieved Frank's mind to see Justin look away, both from the stare and from Mara.

## THIRTY-TWO

Charlemagne parked their armored flash car outside the Fayette Nam Bar and Grill and walked in expensively dressed and obviously packing.

Jay and Skosh parked a small grey government car two blocks down and slunk into the bar looking like government employees drawing per diem. The place was crowded with other government employees, the kind who wear uniforms.

"Special Forces?" asked Skosh.

Jay nodded. "According to Frank, we're a stone's throw—well, maybe a rocket launch—from Smoke Bomb Hill."

Which meant nothing to Skosh, but he did not seek enlightenment.

"What crazy enemy intelligence agent is going to brave this crowd?" he asked.

Jay shrugged. "The kind who wants a beer. I don't know, do I? All that spy v. spy stuff is in your bailiwick tonight. I'm here for the gangstas."

And he saw plenty of those, mostly Cosa Nostra, but a few vory, with their tattooed fingers and dead eyes. There was an occasional interaction between the two groups, a coming and going that suggested a negotiation in progress. Jay was a fan of negotiations that prevented or halted gang wars. Treaties that set up collaboration schemes were not so welcome.

The kinds of collaboration favored by rival gangs involved theft at best, but more often mayhem, extortion, and the maiming and death of innocents. Instinct told him this was not a peace treaty in progress. Representatives from too many disparate gangs without histories of conflict were participating in these talks. They were discussing an alliance. This conclusion did not make him happy.

Skosh found his own reasons for pessimism. The eastern side of the barroom contained an unhealthy number of GRU operatives he recognized from pictures in the files he studied every night in a continuing effort to learn his unwanted promotion. He had never believed in the end of the Cold War. To him, it seemed no more than a continuation on new terms. One of those new terms appeared to be the freedom of foreign military intelligence operatives to enjoy convivial evenings with their American counterparts in a bar outside the southern gate of an army special forces base. Sovereign house or not, he didn't like it.

The two agents stood side by side, conspicuously, at the point where the entrance opened into a large room filled with tables. The name 'bar and grill' was not entirely accurate unless packets of peanuts and potato chips might be considered grill. It was a drinking establishment, nothing more.

They spied their charges at a back table on the left.

"You think they're shielding Mara by not letting her come here?" asked Skosh, surveying the room. Even the wait staff were men.

"Donovan has an expression for your question," said Jay. "Ya think? Of course, they are protecting her. Wouldn't you?"

There was a time when Skosh might have agreed, but he had helped with the beach cleanup of Gennady, the GRU babysitter's body. The ballistics were clear about whose gun it had been. He shivered at the memory.

Jay looked at him sideways. "Yes. I know," he said. "My watcher told me how she went after Gennady. It makes me shudder, too. She appears so soft but is as hard as her brother. Still, I helped rescue her last year, and I would do it again in a flash minute."

Skosh nodded. "Let's go see what they want from us."

Evidently nothing. Misha ordered drinks, to be nursed through an evening of watching and listening, to the room at large and the occasional visits at their table by a wide selection of characters, some sycophants, others carrying a nameless grudge. Skosh recognized a man visiting a table of Cosa Nostra and was sure he was doing his best impression of the inscrutable Asian until Mack said, "That one, then. Tell us at the safehouse."

An older man with gnarled fingers and a sparse comb-over came to their table. His visit proved more interesting—or terrifying—depending on point of view.

Mack initiated the conversation. "Who, on Tuesday nights?"

The man was cautious, which meant he knew the man who had asked the question. "Um. Tuesdays? Um." He closed his eyes to improve his memory. "That would be… that was.…" Skosh fig-

ured he was deciding if he could safely lie. "Um…
Johnny, my son-in-law." He had decided on truth.
Then hurriedly, "He probably didn't understand."

"Are you telling me you are responsible, Oscar?" The stillness of that purring question required no answer, so Mack posed another. "And
Friday nights as well?"

The answer was written in a wide-eyed look
of alarm.

"Is your daughter at home now?"

"No. She works.…"

"Are there children?"

The man gazed at his hands and shook his
head.

…

Jay had the unenviable pleasure of riding back to
the safehouse squashed in the back of the Mercedes between the delinquents, as Skosh called
them. Skosh was meeting the police chief at the
little house with a wide front porch where a young
man tragically fell down the narrow stairs and
broke his neck. By order of Mack, who took a betrayal of trust more seriously than most, the deceased's father-in-law discovered the accident and
reported the death. By now, Skosh was able to recognize Steve's work in the death, and Charlie's in
the bruising.

# THIRTY-THREE

"I don't see how I can find this guy," Justin said as Skosh walked through the dining room door. "Computer searches don't produce anything when there's no name, no place, and no description besides tall and thin."

Everybody was already at the table with full mugs of coffee. Justin told truth to power in his usual reckless way and received the expected menacing glares.

"About that...." Skosh stood in the doorway and felt the heat of unwanted attention shift to him. "It may be nothing, but the police chief told me a story tonight that makes that description interesting."

"First, the man you recognized at the bar," said Mack. "Was he one of the Asian men at the front of the room?"

Skosh nodded. "They were boryokudan—what is called yakuza in the West. Gangsters. He's an enforcer, a muscle guy, named Murakami. Whoever else was at that table, must have been important."

Mack nodded. "Now tell us what the chief told you."

All eyes, among them the four icy blues, were upon him so he took the seat next to Jay and began.

"I told the chief something along the lines of, 'It's a pretty straightforward accident,' meaning the son-in-law. He looked at me and said, 'The fact that you're here makes it anything but straightforward, and I already had one of those iffy kinds this week, so my quota is getting full up.'

"Then he told me about a woman who died in a car wreck three months ago." Skosh waited for snorts and eye rolls, but there were none, making him wonder if he was finally respected or if Mack already knew about this and was patiently waiting for his monologue to end. He pressed on.

"She owned a small newspaper in the next county. The woman had been to Poynter and was a serious journalist. Her paper made a reasonable profit, concentrating on local crime, business, and politics. She had begun running a series of articles about the relationship between one of the small-town city councils and a business looking to move into the area. After the second article, her car went off the road and wrapped around a light pole and she died."

Skosh was becoming more than moderately concerned that he had their rapt attention. He resumed. "The woman's husband, Keith, vowed to carry on the business in her memory and managed to bring out another pair of articles about the new business when he received a threat of sorts. This was according to one of the adult children who told the chief about it, but his searchers couldn't find any sign of it and the daughter had not paid close attention to what the father mentioned almost in passing.

"Then last week, Keith shot himself. The chief lives out that way so he responded to help out because the sheriff's office is short-staffed. He did all the initial interviews and told me three things concerning the case that bothered him. First, the missing threat letter. Second, everybody was adamant that Keith did not own a gun. The gun used in the suicide was unregistered. If he was concerned about the threat, which the chief thought plausible, why go to the trouble of finding something unregistered when he could easily walk into his local gun shop?"

Skosh took a deep breath. "The chief's third concern is the reason I am bringing this up. Two days before the suicide, a neighbor saw Keith in a heated argument with a man outside the front door. The man was tall and thin. The neighbor told the chief she thought the man had limited use of one arm because of the way he opened his car door. She didn't get a plate number but thought the car was grey or silver.

"The newspaper folded before the funeral, without finishing the article series."

"Danny said Liability Man was tall with a long face and a sore arm," said Steve. "I didn't see anybody like that tonight. I did see too many obvious gangsters. Since when do they enjoy the privileges of a sovereign house?"

Charlie took off his already loosened tie and sat back in his chair. "Oscar's son-in-law, Johnny, told us the man used the name Earnest, but he did not know if it was his first or last name. His right arm did not move correctly. He paid Johnny handsomely to take those nights off."

Mack looked at the two sitting by the computers and raised an eyebrow. Mara and Justin grinned at each other, turned, and clicked their keyboards like they were in a race. Sergei scowled.

In five minutes, the race became a collaboration with the two of them putting their heads together in deep consultation. Sergei's scowl deepened. Skosh tried to get Jay's attention, but he was busy asking Frank a stupid question. He did not relish the role of hero, but there was no help for it. A fraction of a second before Sergei launched himself at the younger FBI agent, Skosh put himself in the way and paid for it in the coin of pain. He used his skill in karate to minimize some of the damage, but Sergei was a dirty fighter and in a blind rage.

Charlie and Steve pulled him off in a desultory fashion, and Skosh used the table to haul himself to his feet. He realized as he caught Mara's eye that she was concerned, not about him and his bleeding nose, but about the rising jealousy in Sergei. The man was fucking insane. Well, they were all fucking insane. And they were all too very capable of doing real damage in their insanity. As he brought his head down after staunching the flow from his nose, he saw thoughtful looks all around, all except for Justin, happily tapping his keyboard in total oblivion to the danger he had been in or the debt he owed his reluctant guardian angel. Skosh resolved to enlighten him later.

In five minutes Mara produced a name, John Earnest, an address in Fayetteville, and a company name, Brighton Associates. He was chief financial officer of the company. She turned back to her keyboard to find more information.

It was Justin who caused a profound silence.

"Um. Jay?"

"What is it?"

Justin stared at the screen on the FBI computer. "I can't get in," he said quietly. "It's protected."

"What's protected? Him or the company?"

"Both."

"By…?"

"By us. Or more precisely, by the Criminal Investigation Division."

"Protected?" said Jay. "Or blocked?"

"Protected."

"What does that mean, Jay?" asked Skosh on behalf of everyone in the room.

"John Earnest must be one of ours."

## THIRTY-FOUR

Skosh did not think someone as dark as Jay could visibly pale, but the man took on an ashy hue. His face lost all color and animation.

"Was Sally working for the FBI?" asked Frank. "Could the boy have made a mistake?"

Mack glowered at him. "There was no mistake."

Jay shook his head. "I've never heard of him. Where did he come from?"

"I don't know," said Justin. "I can't find him anywhere in the system. Even if the operation were blocked, he should be in the system, unless the name is a legend or codename."

"Of course, it's a legend," said Jay. "But I don't even recognize the description. Tall, thin, and with an arm injury. Nobody. I do not know him."

Into an unbroken silence dropped a soft, accented voice.

"I know him," said Sergei. "He is on Semianov's list."

"I know every name on that list," said Jay hotly. "There is no Earnest."

"He is Paul Crutchfield on the list. I have met him."

"Crutchfield died in a house fire last winter. He...."

"He is very good with languages," said Sergei. "Though he is a murderer, we put his talent to good use. His real name is Victor Borodinov. Crutchfield and Earnest are two of his game names. He must not see me."

Frank asked, "So he's an illegal?"

Sergei nodded.

"And SVR, not GRU?"

Sergei nodded again. "Also he is a vor, but not a killer. He went to prison because he killed a man he thought was fucking his girlfriend, but he is not a killer. He is well educated and has achieved rank."

"And Arkady from the embassy?"

"Also SVR now and was in my directorate. He is a killer."

The quiet purr from the head of the table was directed at Sergei. "We have made it known we are here," said Misha, tilting his head to one side. "Why must Borodinov not see you?"

It took Sergei time to formulate his reply with just the right words. "He killed the wrong man."

He squirmed under Mara's glare.

...

"Army guy," said Steve.

The two words halted an hour-long argument in full swing. It had taken him a while to bring it to the front of his memory after Skosh's succinct list, taken from Danny's copious notes, of the men making it a regular habit to call on his dim, pretty ex-wife Sally. The GRU guy, the killer SVR guy, the non-killer SVR guy aka Liability Man aka Earnest/Crutchfield/Borodinov, the vor Nick. Danny had mentioned another, Steve knew, because he asked. He and Sally had been divorced for almost a decade and it still pissed him off. He wracked his brain for the memory of his son's words.

"Danny said something about an Army guy. He insisted it was somebody in uniform."

Much of the discussion began to center around the question of why. Why were so many interested in Sally? Why, again, did they all want to eliminate Danny? Why did Borodinov's mission feel more dangerous than the others? And now, who was Army Guy?

Justin came up with another precocious question. "Why protect Borodinov and his business?

We know they're not part of the Bureau. If our people are working on this, the information should be blocked, not just protected."

Sergei inadvertently hit upon part of the answer. "You are asking us to distinguish between two English words. It is unfair."

"You have nailed it, Pavlenko," said Jay. "The people who placed the protection did not know the difference. They are not Bureau."

"And they are in your computer, Sir," said Mara.

Jay lost again the little color he had regained and so failed to recognize the mark of respect Mara had given him. Specialists were rarely polite to their minders, let alone respectful.

"They will know how you live," said Mara, "your family, the results of your last polygraph, your financial records."

"They cannot know all of that," Jay insisted.

"If I can, they can." Mara's quiet ambiguity and the stillness with which she delivered the statement would have made even Steve shiver if he were not so used to it in her father and brother.

"Call your family," said Mack. "Send them to your escape hatch. Then I must use the secure line."

...

The watches began at midnight with perimeter checks, squabbles over rooms, and grumbling.

Skosh knew having plenty of everything would never stop the sniping and complaining. These were as essential to any operation as coffee.

"Listen, Justin," he said as they each staked out space in one room. "You might want to be more careful about how you act with Mara. Especially around her husband."

"Husband?" Justin seemed genuinely puzzled.

"Yeah. Husband. The unhinged killer with the colorless eyes is her husband. How did you not know that?"

"I knew they had something going, but I didn't think they were married."

"You knew they were a couple and you still got as close as you could?"

"All's fair, as they say. I didn't see a ring." Justin smiled. "But if they're married, I guess I'm out."

Skosh blinked. "You know," he formed his next words as slowly and precisely as he could, "even though we're in a nice house with a Mercedes in the garage and good food and coffee, this is not Kansas anymore, don't you?"

"Why would it be Kansas? It's North Carolina."

Skosh used his thumb and forefinger to press his eyes closed. "I mean, Justin, that the world you and I know as normal—though frankly, my family had a lot of that illusion dispelled during the war

—that world, the one with police and grocery stores and streetlights and Thanksgiving Day—that world is not this world. This world is guns and knives and no sleep and bad coffee and people who want to kill you and know how to do it. Our jobs, yours and mine, require us to keep this world at bay so that other people can live in that world thinking all is well. We deal in chaos to keep it away from civilization."

Justin looked puzzled.

Skosh tried emphasis. "Chaos—bad. Civilization—good. This place is chaos. Fair does not exist in chaos. So any rules of civilization you think there are concerning things women—and other luxuries—do not apply here, whether they're married or not. Don't even look at one of their women. Don't even look at a woman you suspect they are looking at. You will get hurt. I got hurt for you today. I'll not get in the way of that again. I promise you."

"So that's why you guys are so careful around them?" asked Justin. "You know, early on I decided against ribbing Steve about his eyelashes. I guess I got too familiar with all the joking and tediously detailed intelligence." His eyes opened wide. "Sergei was coming after me today, is that what you're saying? Thanks. I mean it, but let me take my licks."

Skosh shook his head. "I'd be glad to, but I didn't do it for you. I did it for the computer. You're going to help us find Army Guy tomorrow. You need to be alive to do that."

## THIRTY-FIVE

Everybody—specialist, babysitter, and agent alike—wished the food could always be this good but knew better.

"How did you manage to find these caterers for me, Jay?" asked Skosh through a mouthful of home potatoes.

Mack curled his upper lip when potato bits escaped Skosh's fork.

Jay tilted his head and smiled. "Southern cooking, pal."

"Yeah, well, Florida's in the south...."

This was the closest anyone got to a peaceful non-operational conversation that morning.

Justin and Mara sat side by side at the end of the table where they could turn their seats easily to the computers. They chatted over toast and bacon until Sergei and Steve came in from their generous three hours of sleep.

Sergei pulled Justin out of his chair and to the floor, sweeping his plate after and on top of him.

Despite what Skosh considered to have been a successful explanation and warning the night before, Justin took the bait. He came up swinging.

Jay shouted, "Goodwin!" but there was no simultaneous admonition from Mack, who took a sip of his coffee and watched.

"Your subordinate requires instruction," he said to Jay.

"And you are content to let Pavlenko provide it?"

Because that was what he was doing, blow after blow. Jay knew better than to interfere and possibly make it worse.

"I am," said Mack. And he took another sip.

But Mara was not so content. She placed a dainty hand on Sergei's arm as it was poised to drive again into Justin's belly.

I imagine, thought Skosh, she delayed so long because, like Jay, she knows her intervention can make it harder for Goodwin. He looked at Mack. Maybe that was his reason as well. No, it wasn't. He was savoring his coffee. He just didn't care.

Skosh sighed and made himself unhealthily noticeable by picking the young agent up off the floor and dragging him to the downstairs bathroom for first aid. Jay met them there.

"What the fuck, Goodwin?"

The f-word from Jay? Things were serious.

Goodwin could not answer. Swollen lips, flowing nosebleed, and bruised ribs prevented speech. He did glare daggers at his boss, probably feeling innocent, which was true in the moment before the attack, but only in that moment.

"I think we should separate the computers," said Skosh. "Opposite sides of the table."

*Or planet.*

Justin managed a painful squeak. "We share a modem."

"We'll get longer cables," said Jay. "And you won't speak to her, smile at her, or look at her. Is that clear?"

More daggers, but Justin nodded.

A meeting was in progress when they returned. The detritus of breakfast, dirty plates, platters, crusts of bread, butter wrappers, butter smears, and spilled coffee littered the table. Sergei smirked as Skosh and Jay cleared the mess and Justin sat painfully in his chair, carefully not looking in Mara's direction.

"Alex spoke to Danny about Army Guy," said Mack. "The boy saw him only one time, as he watched from the upstairs landing while the man spoke to Sally just inside the front door. He wore a camouflage uniform and was wide. That is the word Danny used, not fat. Also, he was not much taller than Sally, with closely cut grey hair and no hat. Danny watched again from the front bedroom window while the man climbed into the passenger side of a dark sedan at the curb."

"Senior officer," said Steve. "Because of the grey hair and he must have a car and driver. Did Danny say anything else?"

"They kissed."

"Peck on the cheek? Deep French kiss? What?"

"Alex was his interrogator. She would not ask such a thing. I think an older man visiting Sally would not be content with a peck on the cheek. Her father is still in Colorado."

Was Mack being humorous, or at least sarcastic? Skosh studied the impassive face until the blue eyes turned to him. There was the suggestion of a hint of a shadow of a twinkle. Skosh marveled, then remembered Mack had just spoken to Alex. This could be considered a good mood.

"Sounds like an O-6 or higher," said Jay. He turned to Justin. "Look at all commanders at Fort Bragg who are full colonels or general officers. Also, check Pope Air Force Base. Under six feet, stocky build, grey hair, probably Army but Air Force also sometimes wear BDUs."

...

By the end of the meeting, with all currently attainable information in place, including Skosh's earlier recognition of the Asian gangster, the true tedium began, with multiple surveillance assignments targeting senior commanders, to be followed after dark by a pub crawl and a burglary. Skosh would help with the nighttime burglary of Brighton Associates. Justin would accompany the delinquents on the pub crawl. When Skosh mentioned his concern about this to Frank and Jay, he was told in no uncertain terms to bring it up with Mack himself if he was all that worried; they certainly would not. Skosh decided he was not all that worried.

# THIRTY-SIX

Special Agent Justin Goodwin nursed his third beer of the evening, standing in the smoky recesses of their third bar of the evening, watching his companions become increasingly touchy and hyper-vigilant.

"What are we looking for again?" asked Steve for the hundredth time, though Justin knew damn well the man had the description of their quarry burned into his brain.

"Middle-aged, stocky build, grey hair, buzz cut, eye for the ladies." Justin recited it like a litany and noticed Sergei silently mouthing the words with him. "Three finalists from today's stake-outs, two Army, one Air Force. We're looking for the one...."

Steve interrupted him. "The one who wanted to, and probably did, fuck my ex-wife. Yeah, yeah, yeah I know. Shit, everybody wanted to do that. Hell, I wanted to."

And more in that vein. Justin gathered it was a sore subject.

"Speaking of the ladies," Steve said as he stepped into the path of an attractive young woman. "Hi. What's your name?"

As pickup lines go, it was lame in the extreme. Justin might have said so but was interrupted in the thought by a large man who stepped up close and personal into Steve's face.

"What's it to you, pretty boy?" said the man. "You must be an Air Force toad to have such girly eyelashes."

Sergei muttered, "Shit."

"You must be a grunt to have such a sloped forehead," said Steve.

Of course, the big man had no chance. Though Justin had been on the receiving end of some of Steve's skills, he could not believe the speed with which he brought the man down.

In the parking lot, amid a plethora of expletives, Sergei lamented the hopelessness of their task. "It is impossible. How many bars are there in an Army town?" He shoved Steve into the back seat and climbed in front.

Justin started the car but hunched over his hands, side by side at the top of the wheel. "I think we're on the wrong track."

"Ya think?" said Steve. "We were the oldest guys in there. Most of them weren't even twenty-five."

Justin wanted to tell him to speak for himself but had learned wisdom in the last few hours. He remembered his dad after the divorce, his desperate loneliness, the drinking, and the DUI charge. He'd been arrested coming home from a hotel bar. Nothing fancy, just a haunt of the mid-level business traveler, the fading beauty, and the occasional whore. He headed for one of those hotels lining the highway, three in a row.

They scored at the first hotel lounge. The quarry was there and so was Mack. He sighed as they pulled up chairs and sat down at the little round table that held his beer. "You were unsuccessful."

"And you were not," said Sergei. He received a raised eyebrow in warning.

"Did you fight?"

"Of course," said Steve. There was some reluctance in the admission.

"How many did you vanquish?"

"One."

"Justin pulled us out before others could join," said Sergei.

More raised eyebrows, but these seemed to indicate respect, though Justin might have been mistaken.

Mack sipped his beer. "Which of you thought to look here?"

Justin felt himself blush as Steve tilted his head toward him. Mack's regard was disturbing even when not negative.

"This is my first beer," he said. "The target is on his third whiskey—neat—since I arrived."

"Target?" said Justin.

The blue eyes—no, it was the stillness of the stare not the color—made Justin regret the question.

"He is at an end," said Mack. "If Borodinov does not kill him, I will. He knows this and his remedy is whiskey."

"He knows about you?"

"He knows there is always retribution for betrayal."

"He betrayed Borodinov?"

"He is about to. Our enemy has been too slow. If he knows we are here, he thinks we are searching in noisy bars where young soldiers look for pretty women. You, I mean the three of you—why English has no distinct plural in the second person familiar is a mystery—you helped to reinforce this impression. Borodinov does not know what we have in the young Special Agent Goodwin."

He received three blank stares and continued. "First, Goodwin limited the necessary public display so that a major bar brawl did not make us as slow as Borodinov. Then, he thought of something other than pretty women for just enough time to know where to find a disappointed middle-aged man. And now, he will use his credential to convince the colonel to accompany him quietly."

Mack rose. "I have parked the Mercedes on the west side of the building, Agent Goodwin. We will meet you there.

## THIRTY-SEVEN

"I don't understand why I'm going with you instead of one of the FBI agents who could stop an arrest with the flash of a badge," said Skosh. "I don't carry credentials. Company policy."

"They are all about law and order," said Mara. "You are about lawlessness and disorder, at least in other countries."

Skosh watched the blonde head next to him shine on and off under the flash of passing streetlights until he caught himself nearly running a red light and slammed down on the brakes. He wondered how anybody so adorably cute could be so fucking deadly.

"All we need is for you to drive, Nakamura," said the icicle in the back seat. More like a vast expanse of treeless tundra back there.

"Charlie, please be civil," said Mara.

"There's nothing civil in what we do, Mara."

"But we can treat each other in a civil manner."

"I dispute that Skosh qualifies as part of 'each other.' Your husband does not think any of these people qualify, judging by the way he pounds his fist into them, especially Goodwin. Does he interest you?"

"I don't want to discuss it," said Mara.

"Every private thought belongs to the team. Do not forget that. We will discuss it." Then, after a lengthy pause, "But not here."

While Skosh waited for Charlie and Mara to finish breaking and entering, he allowed his mind to wander over the revelation that there were no private thoughts on the team. How did such a rule come about? How was it enforced? Why was it necessary? As an intelligence officer, Skosh was aware that his mores often resembled those of the slightly thoughtful criminals he had met and sometimes had the misfortune to work with. His official enemies in the game came equipped with a moral compass similar to his own. Sure, there were arrests, accidents, betrayals, even the occasional murder, but what kind of survival imperative would outlaw private thoughts?

Speaking of survival imperatives, Mara and Charlie had been gone too long. Skosh's dislike of the blue metal building five hundred feet away on a downward slope from where he was parked burgeoned into loathing.

A small white door had been set in one corner. No windows. Who ever heard of an 'Associates' headquartered in a metal barn with no windows? Associates belonged in offices, with secretaries, nursery-provided potted plants, a parking lot with lines painted on it, and above all, windows.

He got out of the car quietly, closed and locked it, then stepped to the edge of the trees sheltering him and the car. He was about to step out and begin a quiet walk toward the looming metal box of a building before him when a female voice to his right whispered, "Get back to the car."

"Where is Charlie?"

"He is inside, listening, but cannot get out. Use the car phone to call Frank. Tell him we dare not use our transmitters. They have extensive security and a scanner. It is a meeting. About fifteen people. At least five are fighters, but all are armed. Tell him to reach the rest of the team. You will have to meet them and bring them here. There is not much cover."

"Come with me."

"No. Do as I say, damn it. I have the authority here and will make your life a misery if you do not follow my orders. I need the team here now. This minute. Go, and be fucking quiet about it."

...

Skosh revised his definition of adorably cute as he waited for the Mercedes to pull up next to him at a gas station half a mile from Brighton Associates. While he waited, he noticed a shop front across the street with a for sale sign and 'News Courier Times' painted on the window.

## THIRTY-EIGHT

When Michael heard the scanner, he stopped in mid-sentence. "Go get...." Their system was shielded but the scanner would pick up an unidentified signal and spark a need to investigate.

"Help," said Mara.

He had to depend on her ability to interpret his sudden stop. That she answered correctly with just one word finishing his thought, then cut her mic heartened him. He had been about to cut the throat of the mammoth looming in front of him but thought better of it. With Mara gone, no ability to communicate, and the team not yet here, he could not risk discovery of an inexplicable bloodless corpse. A search would not be good for him right now.

He slipped behind the sentry and up a supporting pillar studded with narrow footholds leading into the metal support structure of the roof. It was an ordinary metal building, painted navy blue on the outside, but left raw on the inside, with a cement floor and no niceties like air conditioning or even windows in the late summer heat of North Carolina. Roll-up garage doors at the north and south ends of the building had been left open ten inches, presumably to provide airflow, but the measure failed to give relief to anyone but the mosquitoes who feasted on the sweltering bodies inside. At least the tangos could swat at them, setting up a continuous slap-slap tattoo. Michael could do nothing but contribute blood to the nutritional needs of the species. Occasionally, he passed a slow hand under his nose or chin to stop the sweat from dripping onto the man standing below.

The space inside echoed with voices and scraping chairs as ten men sat around three long folding tables pushed together to make a conference table. A large safe stood against the wall near a corner with two tall filing cabinets and a small table holding a coffee maker.

The meeting resembled every business gathering Michael ever had attended, methodical, tedious, and tense. That it was populated by representatives of various criminal entities made no difference in the dynamic resemblance to an intelligence planning group. Borodinov steered the discussion almost as well as Misha would. When he left them, citing another engagement, Michael hoped someone was still outside to track him. He was about to risk a word to Mara, but the gathering devolved into professional sniping among the criminals as they closed briefcases rich with information, pushed their chairs back, and prepared to leave.

At the same time, his earbud came alive, suddenly and briefly. Four brief sound bursts as of someone tapping a transmitter. He recognized it. Papa had made them memorize Morse Code as children, against their many objections. It was so old-fashioned. Four dots: H. Mara was here, back with the team. He did not hear the signal come through on the scanner below. It was too brief to pick up and the breakup of the meeting was too noisy.

Michael considered carefully how to communicate what he knew they needed as unambiguously as possible. He tapped a dot and two dashes on the transmitter at his belt. W. He was on the west side of the building. He waited fifteen seconds before sending the next. D for *Dach* in German then waited two beats and followed with R for roof in English. Five beats, S, *sofort*, then N for now. He repeated S, then heard, in the clear, Sergei giving the channel for detonation and his father giving the order, "*Sofort*."

Then, the center of the roof and the roll-up doors at each end exploded.

…

Mara was not pleased by their excessive protectiveness. They conspired to deny her an equal role, coming up with lame excuses or far-fetched scenarios, trying to make her assigned task seem more important than it was. Her stepfather was the worst, but her husband came in a close second. Michael and Steve were more hard-nosed and modern in their approach, but they did nothing to support her. This time, Steve went so far as to say out loud, "Shut the fuck up, Mara."

She seethed as she set the charge in the center of the roof and ran back to her position in the southeast corner next to Misha. He handed her the gauntlets she would use to slide down the rope to the floor of the building thirty feet below. Then he donned his own. She set the receiver frequency of the detonator on hearing a single word from Sergei, who spoke it aloud in everybody's ear after Michael's first S code became clear and imperative. Sergei had put the packages together, calculating the blast requirements for the partially open roll-ups and the steel-supported roof.

They were not separate blasts. They were a single blast, cubed. Sergei was that precise. Misha gave the order and dropped through the hole, even while the debris was still airborne. Mara measured the distance behind him and followed him into a gun battle, arriving almost on top of him. Why hadn't he rolled? He was firing long bursts from his MP5, covering her, but he did not stand.

Mara took two rounds in her armored vest, they made her spin and stole some of her breath, but she responded instinctively. She stood, giving herself the slightest advantage over Misha's position on the floor. Their mutual target, the one pinning Misha and coming ever closer to hitting her somewhere lethal, was to their left. Because she was standing, Mara could see the top of his head beyond the large safe. Bad angle, maybe two square inches of target, but plenty for her. It was this guy's bad luck that Louis had been her teacher. Mara's was the last shot fired.

...

Misha watched the colonel's body roll into a ditch. The man would not appreciate his pity, so he had been careful to conceal it. Steve proved himself once again as a master interrogator. The colonel told them everything without violence.

All Steve said to him was, "So Colonel, how's it feel to be a traitor?" The forest they stood in under dripping leaves became the man's confessional. They were his three priests. Misha's SIG administered penance and the man took it as absolution.

Half an hour later, most of that time spent barreling down country roads after Skosh's urgent call, they stood under more dripping trees while he dressed Mara in the tactical gear they had brought with them. Misha was pleased to see Sergei bend himself to the task before him after giving Skosh an initial evil eye. The man knew explosives. It was good to have this capability again after the loss of Vasily. A loss aided by Sergei. The thought made Misha's jaw clench.

As he watched Sergei work, he appreciated his son-in-law's ability to quell the demons in his own private hell surrounding Mara. He knew that hell. He and Louis had nearly killed each other in the one surrounding Alex. Steve was careful, never looking at either Mara or Alex, but Misha knew it was Alex who interested him the most and always had since the day he met her in Chicago after Vasily's death. He was younger than she was, but not by enough to make Misha comfortable.

Michael was settled with Theresa, thanks to Alex, though she did not know why he had approved her project. It wasgood for the team and must now be extended to Steve, but Misha had no earthly idea how to go about it. He dared not ask his wife. It would call her attention to the man who did his best to remain invisible to her. He appreciated Steve's discretion. Of course, Misha would probably kill him otherwise, so he had incentive not to let his glance linger too long. For now, the only practical solution was for Alex not to become a widow again until she was too old to interest anyone.

For the first time in his life, Misha felt required to live.

But he also required his daughter to live, which was why he peremptorily quashed her bid to be the first down the rope into the midst of a firestorm. She was unhappy. So was he. This was more than an operation; it was a situation. Every junction was murky, every decision a choice between evils, every step precarious. And now his mortality had become another enemy.

As he slid down the rope, he could think of only one word when he felt the impact on his left hip. It was Steve's word.

*Fuck.*

...

Justin sat in Skosh's rental car parked under the trees with the other three government men staring down at the building below. The sky had begun to brighten in preparation for dawn, but there was no cheer in the light. A miserable soaking drizzle had set in, making the windshield wipers necessary. It leaked through windows they had cracked open in an effort to breathe. The mosquitoes followed the rain so that within the car the silence was broken by random slapping sounds from all four occupants.

From outside the car, after the initial explosions, came the sounds of popping gunfire, in steady single shots and short bursts. It had been going on for two minutes. Too long, according to Frank.

The firing stopped and a form streaked toward them running at full speed from the building. With one mind, they all climbed out and stood in the rain, their hands on their weapons, loosened in their holsters but not drawn. The figure was fast, very fast, but small. And blonde, without the Kevlar hood.

She managed to say, "Ambulance," when within earshot, gasping as she closed the remaining distance.

"We have them standing by," said Skosh. "How many?"

"One."

Her face streamed with water. It was difficult to tell in the murky light, but Justin was sure she was crying. The clue was in the way she gasped for air.

"Who and how bad?" said Frank.

"Misha. It's bad."

"The tangos?"

"All dead. Except one. We will explain the intelligence we found later. This is not over. Borodinov is missing."

…

Skosh faced off with the new leader of Charlemagne straight away.

"The man is in agony, for God's sake!" He knew he was shouting. He knew how dangerous was the man he shouted at, and how dangerous was the man in agony on the gurney between them. He did not care. Mack's breathing was a series of gasps produced to take the place of screams.

The FBI's emergency surgeon stood at the head of the gurney, holding a walloping dose of morphine drawn up in a syringe and ready to go. Skosh shouted again, echoes bouncing off the walls of the hangar. "I don't give a fuck about your fucking policies, Charlie. Stop being such a fucking hard ass and let him have some relief. Be human for a change. He's your father, damn it!"

There was an audience of… everybody. They stood around in a solemn clot of filthy, tired, dispirited people, too exhausted even to shuffle their feet. Charlie answered without shouting and it was worse, not just because of the underlying venom, but because of his hyper-rationality at a time when anybody else would be, should be, raving.

"I owe you no explanation, Skosh. At your insistence, I allowed the X-ray to delay us. Each moment you shout at me delays us. You, not I, have added to his agony." Charlie paused, visibly leashing his temper. "He will receive the morphine after I have had a chance to speak with him privately. He needs relief; I require his mind; Charlemagne's exigency elevates my requirement over his need. It is my call. I have made it. Get out of our way or I will shoot you here. Now."

The words were scary enough. The ice-cold low tone took that adjective off the charts. The threat did not make Skosh step aside, though he knew it looked that way. It was the glimpse into Charlie's calculated thinking, the revelation that the team had the ultimate claim. Their lives were hell. He was glad they were going home, finished or not. He needed a break from their Gehenna.

Then he was told to board the airplane.

## EPILOGUE

Jay had never flown first class before. Charlemagne let them off at Reykjavik and insisted on giving them first-class tickets home. Charlie's threat briefing during the flight also had been first class.

For too many reasons, the first thing Jay would do in Chicago would be to arrange Goodwin's transfer to his office. The computer skills would be handy of course, but more important was what Jay had discovered at Reykjavik.

Frank did not get off the airplane. More than that, he had been asked, in Jay's hearing, if he had any messages for Maryann and Theresa. They were radioing ahead. To their lair. And to Maryann. Even after this present gargantuan threat was eliminated, Frank and his wife would be irreparably tainted by what Jay referred to as TMK, too much knowledge.

Almost as bad, because the young agent knew too much without actually understanding Frank's situation, Goodwin had a mild case of the same. Jay had it, too, of course, but enjoyed enough insight and experience to bury it deep. Goodwin, on the other hand, did not even know he was infected. Jay would keep him under his thumb for as long as it took to enlighten him.

Meanwhile, his own family would have to stay in the escape hatch. In a month's time, only luck and the skills of Charlemagne would determine if they could come home.

...

Justin asked for a martini, shaken, not stirred. He got an iced concoction of vermouth and vodka in a squat glass. So much for first class. He drank it too fast, making his head spin and the salted nuts important in keeping his stomach down.

Chicago. He had been there once, as a boy. His dad had put the boat on Lake Michigan and taken him along the shoreline. The place was huge, the price of gas for the engine astronomical, and the wind incessant. He'd had a bad sunburn. But it became one of the happiest memories of his childhood. Maybe they could go fishing next summer if Dad was up to it.

Winter would be a bitch, though.

…

The good news was Skosh was finally going home and would have a decent plate of sushi in about a month. Mack might live, and they had hauled in a shit-ton of intelligence as briefed by Charlie.

The bad news was he would not be eating his sushi on the Ginza. Even if he lived, Mack was unlikely to be sufficiently mobile to be active by then, meaning his scary-as-fuck son, the one he had just pissed off in the hangar, would be in charge of the op. And now, Skosh had only a month to coordinate with everybody from the officials of Okinawa Prefecture to the behemoth that was the U.S. Department of Defense.

Before any of that could be addressed, once he landed in North Carolina, he still had several American authorities to placate and an enormous day-old mess to clean up. Just as Skosh was leaving Charlemagne's airplane, Steve put a cherry on top of this cake of horrors by telling him about a colonel lying in a ditch along a country road with one of Mack's bullets in his head.

"He didn't cut the guy's throat?"

Steve shrugged. Skosh waited.

"Maybe he felt sorry for the guy," said Steve.

Skosh had never known pity to be part of a specialist's emotional repertoire.

Steve gave an exasperated snort. "The guy bonked my wife. Okay?"

"Ex. For almost ten years."

"Yeah, well I have a long memory. You might want to consider that, Nakamura."

"So all that great intelligence the colonel provided is going to be visible on the body, probably courtesy of you, and because I didn't know about it until now, already in the local press?"

"No. Not in the press. Brighton shut that down, didn't they? As killers go, they're almost as effective as we are."

"But not quite."

"Let's hope not."

...

Theresa made use of the time it would take the team to fly home by getting acquainted with the surgical room at Vasily's Carpet. She acquired new supplies, threw away obsolete and questionable items, and disinfected and arranged everything in a modern, rational manner. The surgeon who came from Vienna to lead her seemed to approve. It was hard to tell. Was it nationality that made him as dour and stern as Misha, or just a natural consequence of long-unassailed supremacy in his field? The butler had it, too, but he was French, so maybe it was not nationality.

The FBI surgeon on call had managed to slide the gurney under a portable X-ray in a hangar before putting Misha on the airplane, and the FBI radiologist had described in detail the mess he saw. These reports came to Theresa by fax. Her request that Mara and Sergei be rested and alert on landing was sent to the airplane by radio. They would be rested but filthy. Cleanliness would have to be imposed once they walked through the door. Theresa would give them twenty minutes max.

Alex thought she would be helping. Theresa knew better and would leave it up to Michael to handle that. They were not sure Misha would live, let alone regain any kind of mobility. Alex was likely to be a liability.

As the gurney rolled through the door with its heavily sedated occupant, Alex predictably lost her shit. Maryann, obeying a signal from Michael, led her away sobbing. Steve watched her go.

In that instant, Theresa had a vision of life at Vasily's Carpet without that frightening man on the gurney, understood a tenth of the stakes, and began playing her part in the preservation of all their lives by trying to save one.

*The End*

Will Mack survive? Who wants to kill young Danny and why? Find out in the next Charlemagne File, Swallow, available now at your favorite bookstore: https://books2read.com/u/4A2YAp

Join the Charlemagne Files newsletter for more stories and information about the series, its world of covert operations, and the lives of the characters on the team. Sign up here: https://www.charlemagnefiles.com/contact

If you enjoyed this book, please consider leaving a short review at your favorite bookstore.

# CHARLEMAGNE AND THE SECTION

The fictional world of The Section follows a few conventions. It may help the first-time reader of The Charlemagne Files to know some of these.

**Who/what/ where is The Section?**

The Section is a department of an intelligence agency of the United States. Its employees are civil servants. It includes support staff members who provide identity documents, financial controls, and physical and document security. The offices are near the East Coast, maybe Virginia.

The operational agents are called babysitters. They arrange on-site logistical support for freelance specialists during operations. Most operations are not conducted within the United States, with some exceptions.

Babysitters themselves do not carry identity documents in their names during an operation and never carry any official identification from their organization. Their purpose is to allow the organization to deny any association with them or their mission.

**Nicknames**

Babysitters in The Section receive nicknames from their coworkers when they join the office. These names are often undesirable and used mercilessly among the members of the office. It is part of the team-building process in a stressful occupation.

## Coins

Challenge coins are traditionally stamped with symbols or mottos that designate the intelligence unit of their owners. The tradition is that when members of the unit are present at the bar and one produces his coin, all must produce theirs. Anyone failing to show their coin is responsible for the bar tab. If all produce their coins, then the challenger who first produced his or her coin is responsible for the tab.

## File designations

The highest classification of information is Top Secret. Beyond Top Secret, more sensitive information is strictly controlled in a number of ways including designation as Sensitive Compartmented Information (SCI). This requires an additional clearance and often a named clearance based on Need-To-Know.

In The Section, files on specialists or specialist teams receive a one-word code name, printed across the file and restricted to very few people. When a solo or specialist team is employed on an operation, another designator word will refer to the operation and will be used for funding, reports, etc.

The Section's file name for Charlemagne is WEDGE. Thus CETUS WEDGE (second book of the Charlemagne Files) means an operation dubbed CETUS using the team called WEDGE.

## Specialist

A team or solo operative used by Western governments for black operations conducted without fingerprints in high-risk situations expected to involve death.

# GLOSSARY OF GAME NAMES

## <u>Charlemagne</u>

Original Team

Mack: so dubbed by Western babysitters because he uses a knife at times; Austrian leader and decision maker of Charlemagne; called Misha by other members of his team; probable real name is Michael; last name is unknown.

The Frenchman: deceased marksman and technical expert of Charlemagne; real name is Louis; last name is unknown.

Vasily Sobieski: deceased explosives expert and martial artist whose father was a noted solo specialist; no aliases.

Later Team

**Charlie Taylor**: marksman; son of Mack; probable real name is Michael; last name unknown.

**Steve Donovan**: martial artist; former fighter pilot; abandoned real name was Daniel Martin Kessler.

**Mara Sobieski Pavlenko**: technical expert and marksman; daughter of Vasily Sobieski and biological daughter of Mack; wife of Sergei Pavlenko.

**Sergei Pavlenko**: explosives expert; former KGB babysitter; husband of Mara Sobieski.

### Babysitters

**Frank Cardova**: long-time babysitter of Charlemagne; later, head of The Section; real name is Leo Vilseck; Section nickname is Buddy.

**Justin Goodwin**: FBI special agent and IT specialist; no aliases.

**John Nakamura**: official game name; real name unknown; usually called by his Section nickname, Skosh.

**Jay Turner**: FBI counterintelligence agent with a private agenda; no aliases.

### Family members

**Alexandra Sobieski**: widow of Vasily Sobieski and daughter of former Charlemagne babysitter and head of Section Fred Dolnikov; no aliases. Now married to Mack.

**Maryann and Theresa Vilseck:** wife and daughter of Leo Vilseck, aka Frank Cardova.

**Sally and Danny Kessler:** ex-wife of and son of Steve Donovan.

# GLOSSARY OF TERMS

**AK-47** - developed by Mikhail Kalashnikov in 1947, one of the most ubiquitous firearms worldwide. It is reliable, uses standard 7.62 x 39mm ammunition, is inexpensive and fully automatic. Pretty much standard issue for insurgents and terrorists everywhere.

**Babysitter** - a government officer or agent responsible for the care, feeding, and security of a specialist under contract to that government, as well as for the fulfillment of the contract.

**Beretta** - an Italian-made weapon by the oldest continuous firearms manufacturer in the world.

**BDU** - battle dress uniform, loose fitting and designed for terrain camouflage and free range of motion.

**Dangle** - slang for an otherwise uninvolved person used as bait in an operation to trap a target.

**Glock** - semi-automatic pistol manufactured by an Austrian company.

**HK** - Heckler & Koch, a German manufacturer of popular automatic weapons, especially submachine guns and assault rifles.

**M-16** - 5.56 mm American military assault rifle.

**Running point** - a term used in military and business applications to designate the lead in an operation. In a specialist operation, the position requires stealth and silence in removing especially dangerous obstacles such as watchers and snipers.

**SAS** - Special Air Service, the special forces unit of the British Army founded in 1941.

**SCIF** - Sensitive Compartmented Information Facility, a secure facility used by American and British military, security, and intelligence service to process sensitive compartmented information.

**SIG Sauer** - a German Swiss firearms manufacturer.

**Specialist** - an outside operative used by a government in extremely sensitive situations in which death of the opponent is likely and/or desired.

**Tango** - military slang for a hostile operative, usually a terrorist.

**touch** - a listening tap.